SO]
WITCH

MIDLIFE IN MOSSWOOD BOOK 5

louisa west romance

JAN 2022

10.99

MW00647234

SON OF A
WITCH

MIDLIFE IN MOSSWOOD BOOK 5

lw.

LOUISA WEST

For the chosen family in my life.
You know who you are.

I don't think you ever really know what all you're doing, so you have to act on faith.

— DOLLY PARTON

CHAPTER ONE

Birthday parties were supposed to be joyous occasions. Everyone was coming together to celebrate a day that was special to someone they loved. Fun decorations, balloons, and party blowers were the order of the day, and birthday cake was an absolute given. The room was abuzz with people chatting, eager for their own piece of sickly-sweet goodness with extra buttercream frosting. But a storm had just touched down amidst the celebrations, and it seemed to be fixed on destruction.

Hi, Dad.

Declan stood in the eye of that storm, eyes wide and face blank from the revelation. His mouth opened and then closed again like a blowfish, and he turned a paler shade of pasty than usual. Rosie felt like she'd been hit by lightning herself; her nerves rubbed against each other, causing a red-hot type of friction that she didn't know how to calm.

What the actual fuck? She knew Declan had been married, but he'd never said anything about a son. She studied his face, looking for a sign—*any* sign—that he had an inkling about what was going on, but he was staring blankly at the boy. He actually looked like he might be going into shock.

Holy Mother Moon.

The people close enough to hear the kid's sneer were thankfully comprised largely of their nearest and dearest. Rosie's eyes were wide as saucers and she felt her stomach bottom out, the way it always did when she rode in an elevator. She hated riding in elevators, because she always felt like *this* time would be *the* time she'd crash into the basement—the likeness of the two experiences wasn't lost on her. She stood frozen in time, one hand on Maggie's shoulder and the other loosely grasping the knife she had been holding as she prepared to cut the cake.

A gentle touch steadied her hand, before someone took the knife from her.

"Here hon," Tammy said gently, bringing her slowly back to the moment. "I've got this. Why don't you go help Declan?"

It took Rosie a second to register Tammy's diplomatic suggestion. She nodded ignoring the dryness in the back of her throat as she made her way through the crowd to Declan's side. The boy raised a sandy blonde brow as he sized her up, leaning into the arm that towed his suitcase.

"*So* sorry to barge in like this," he began, the scathing lilt of his tone instantly undermining the stiff British quality of his manners. "Turns out my mother never gave my grandparents legal custody of me, so now that she's fucked off I can't stay with them anymore." He glanced between the pair of them again, as though wanting a second look at Rosie before his attention honed in on Declan. "Have you seen her, by the way? Blonde woman, bout this tall. Calls every now and again to complain about you and your prophecy and then I don't hear from her for another couple of months —that one?"

Gemma.

Rosie felt her heart squeeze with panic. Was she still alive? Had she managed to somehow claw her way back from being swallowed by her own dark magic?

Rosie's gaze flicked to Declan, who was already looking at her. Her mouth felt like it was full of sawdust. If Gemma was actually alive, who knows what she might have told people. Would she be looking for revenge? Would she still be looking to steal Rosie's magic by any means possible?

"Rings a bell, I see," the kid snarked, his moss-colored eyes full of anger.

Rosie took a sharp breath as the information flooded her brain—and then glanced briefly at the people around them who might have heard the word *prophecy*.

"If y'all ain't busy," Ben said politely, passing discretely by Declan, "then we sure could use some more soda bringin' out of the back room."

Declan blinked, and then nodded gratefully. "Let's go," he said quietly, moving aside and gesturing with his free hand towards the kitchen door so that Rosie could lead the way. She was happy to oblige, if only because it immediately gave her something to do, but her gaze flicked to the kid. Would he be compliant?

The boy hesitated. His eyes darted between Rosie and Declan, and then to the floor. At last he gave a single, terse nod, and Rosie released the breath she hadn't realized she'd been holding. She forced her feet to move, one in front of the other, as she took them through the kitchen and straight towards the back door before ducking into the back room off the side.

It was little more than a storage closet, and a hectic one at that. She and Tammy had been so rushed getting ready for Nourish's grand opening and Maggie's birthday celebration that an unspoken promise had sprung up between them to tidy up when it was all over. But as Declan and the boy squeezed into the space with her, that promise bit her in the butt. She felt her checks flush with heat as she scrambled to stack a few boxes more neatly, making what little room she could.

But worrying about the state of her storeroom seemed a little redundant when she was immediately joined by a kid Declan never knew he *had*. She accidentally made eye contact with the boy, wanting to really study him for his resemblance to Declan. But a deep pang of guilt took her heart in its icy grip, and Rosie averted her gaze. This was *Gemma's* son—and Gemma had been swallowed up by dark magic and black earth deep in Needlepoint Woods.

Declan pulled the door closed behind him, shutting out any residual noise from the party. Rosie didn't know if that was such a great idea. It suddenly seemed like there wasn't enough air for the three of them. An awkward silence loomed, and Rosie was desperate to fight it off.

"Would you like a soda?" she asked lamely, glancing at the boxes of soda cans stacked on shelves on one side of the room.

"I'm good," the kid replied, setting his jaw.

Declan shuffled closer to the boy, if such a thing was even possible, staring openly. "You're mine?" he asked in awe.

His son squared up bony shoulders that he hadn't grown into yet, clenching his jaw in a way that was so startlingly similar to a pose Declan sometimes adopted that Rosie didn't think there was any denying the family connection. The blonde hair, which had just a tinge of rusty undertone, and eyes the exact shade of green as his father's cemented it.

"Only so far as you're mine," the kid snapped viciously. He fiddled with a silver cigarette lighter in his right hand, flipping it open and lighting it. "Sharing my DNA doesn't make you my *dad*." He snapped the lighter closed when he said the word 'dad'.

When Declan seemed momentarily speechless, the kid lost his patience.

"Look mate," he said, rolling his eyes. He dug into his back pocket for a wad of folded paper. "All I need is for you to sign these emancipation forms, and I'll be out of your hair. Then I can be on my own, like I always have been."

Declan blinked and took the papers that were thrust at him, unfolding and scanning them.

"Gabriel Cillian Forrest," he said out loud, his voice low and slow, like he was mesmerized by those eight syllables.

"Right," the boy scoffed bitterly. "Should have known you wouldn't even know my *name*. Just donated the sperm and then fucked off—typical!"

Declan opened his mouth as though his first instinct was to tell the kid that his language wasn't acceptable, but then stopped himself. Rosie raised a brow, wondering if that was indicative of the kid's standard language, or if he was trying it on because he had no boundaries right now.

"Yeah, my name's Gabriel," he conceded, flicking his blonde mane back out of his face with a jerk of his neck.

"How old are you?" Declan asked, briefly reading through the first page of the papers.

"Fourteen," Gabriel said. "Not that it's any of your business."

"It's my business," Declan answered, looking up from the papers with his brows drawn together, "because you're too young t'be out on ya own." He paused. "Is it even legal for you to be emancipated?"

Gabriel crossed his arms over his chest, one eyebrow tilted. "Don't pretend to care about what happens to me all of a sudden," he said, rolling his eyes.

Declan looked at Rosie, pressing his lips together. Then he refolded the papers, and tucked them into his *own* pocket. "I'm not signing these."

"What?" Gabriel asked incredulously. "You've *got* to be kidding me."

"I'm not makin' any decisions about anythin' when I've only just found out I have a son," Declan declared with a shrug. "Sorry."

Rosie held her breath. Declan glanced from Gabriel to her, and when their eyes met he asked an unspoken question. The real question for Rosie, however, was would they be able to survive this latest issue? After a couple of seconds, she nodded at Declan and then let out her breath in a slow, steady stream.

"Well, Gabriel," Declan said, lifting his brows in a matter-of-fact expression. "I don't know where you were planning on stayin' while you're in town, but we have a couch with your name on it." He met his son's gaze, jade on jade. "If you want it, that is."

FOX COTTAGE WAS DECEPTIVELY PEACEFUL. CRICKETS sang low, soft lullabies in the long grass fringing the woods, accompanying the waxing moon as she crested the tops of the pine trees. Knowing that both kids were asleep should have reassured Rosie as she made her way from the bathroom to the bedroom she shared with Declan, but it didn't. She felt uneasy, like she was being lulled into a false sense of security. Declan was sitting up in bed reading, the covers pulled across his lap and his broad chest looking more tanned than it actually was, thanks to the glow from the bedside lamp.

"Hey you," Rosie said, her affection for him warming her words. It had been a hectic day from sun-up to sun-down, in ways that neither of them had even imagined.

"Hey yourself," Declan replied, putting his book aside and letting his gaze drift lazily over her as she slipped under the covers. "Feel better?"

"Much," she sighed, cuddling up to him. Her arm went automatically around his waist, her cheek to his warm skin. "But how are *you* feeling?"

"Hardly know," he murmured gently. "It's a lot to take in."

She could feel the tension in his abdominal muscles, as though he was ready to leap into action at any moment. Rosie's lips flattened into a worried line.

"I know, hon," she said, her fingers brushing his side

soothingly. "I'm so sorry. But for what it's worth, I think you dealt with it really well."

Declan allowed himself a mirthless chuckle.

"Thanks darlin'," he said, placing a grateful kiss on the crown of her head. "I just wish I knew what *he's* thinkin' about it all now."

Rosie lifted her head a little to peer up at him. "Why don't you take him with you on your route tomorrow? Bonding time?"

"That'll be grand," he smiled back at her. "Thanks for the suggestion."

"No problem. Did you manage to get hold of his grandparents?"

"Yeah," Declan sighed, stroking her arm. "They weren't exactly thrilled to hear from me, but they were pretty glad to know he was safe. He didn't tell them he was plannin' on coming—just left them a note on their kitchen table. He took their credit card and got his plane ticket an' just... left."

"Oh my God," Rosie groaned. "They must have been worried sick!"

"That's puttin' it mildly," Declan confirmed, his voice flavored with sarcasm.

"I mean, the criminal part of what he did aside," Rosie added, "it takes a pretty determined kid to get in a plane and travel halfway across the world to knock on the door of a man he's never met." Her mind whirled in a never-ending Viennese waltz, each loop more dramatic than the last. "Did you have any idea that you had a son?" she asked gently.

"None," Declan promised. "Gemma never mentioned a thing, an' her parents were never fans of mine to begin with. I'm bettin' that they just swallowed whatever lies she fed them," he muttered darkly, before sighing again.

"Gemma and I..." he paused, pressing his lips together as he considered how to best tell the story. "We should never have been together in the first place. We were kids, and I already told you we were both tryin' to upset our parents. When we left Vegas and went back to the UK, her parents forbid her from seein' me again. I'd already pissed off me Da', and she seemed to be glad of the break so we just kind've... went our separate ways. It wasn't a deep relationship."

"It was deep enough that a child was born from it," Rosie pointed out.

Declan shrugged helplessly, frowning at the situation. "But not deep enough for her to want me to be involved in raisin' him, apparently."

After a beat, Rosie addressed the elephant in the room. "Will you sign the papers?"

"Tough question." He leaned his head back against the pillows, looking up at the ceiling as he considered his answer. "It's a bit hard for a bloke to find out he has a son and then sign the kid away in the next breath," he admitted. "I guess I could send him back to his grandparents and get some legal advice about my rights. Unless..."

Declan petered off. With her head resting on his chest, Rosie could hear his heart beating. It was slow and steady, despite the nature of the conversation. Somehow, it helped to ease some of her own worry. Just a little.

"Unless he decides he wants to stay?" she asked, watching the bedroom curtain flutter in the night breeze.

"Would you be okay with that?"

She took a breath, held it for a second, and then released it slowly. "It's a lot to take in. We'd have to think about it as a family—about how we would make it work. But he's your son, and yes—in theory—I'm okay with it."

"Well I won't make any decisions about anything on my own," Declan told her, sounding relieved. "We need to be in this together—no matter which way forward we take."

"Agreed," she said, cuddling a little closer to him.

They both fell quiet. Rosie's mind kept going back to the lies that Gemma had been telling Gabriel his whole life. Whatever Randy's faults had been—and he'd had *plenty*—she would never have lied to and hurt Maggie in that way. She couldn't imagine how Declan was feeling as he tried to make sense of it all while simultaneously accepting that he was now a father.

"Are you okay?" she asked him softly, as though not to shake him out of his thoughts too abruptly.

He seemed to consider her question carefully before giving his answer. "Yeah, I think so." He curled his arm a little tighter around her. "Leastways I don't think what I'm goin' through is anything compared to what he's been through."

"I wouldn't say that," Rosie said. "From one parent to another, finding out that you've created a whole other human is a pretty big deal. You're allowed to have feelings about it."

"Mostly I just feel..." He trailed off, searching for the right word. "*Guilty*. Like I should have known, somehow. Like I should have *been* there."

"You're a witch," Rosie reminded him, "not a psychic. Gemma had plenty of opportunity to tell you— either directly, or by getting in touch with your family— and she chose to keep it to herself."

Declan's arm tightened a little, his muscles flexing with a flash of irritation. "She was always trouble," he muttered darkly. He sighed, letting his head fall back to rest on the headboard. "If I'd known just how *much* trouble she was gonna be, I'd have given her a wide berth."

"Maybe you would have," Rosie agreed, "but none of that changes anything now. Right *now* you need to focus on the fact that there is a young man in your life who needs you. Needs *us*."

Declan smiled. It was a weak, tired version of the expression that tugged at Rosie's heart strings. "You're right, as usual. Thank you, Your Majesty."

She pushed herself up until she could reach his lips with hers. A sweet, lingering kiss passed between them, full of understanding and the faintest hint of hope. "You're welcome, Your Majesty," she smirked before he brushed her bangs, which were getting long, to one side of her face.

"Shall we give in to royal slumber?" Declan asked. "I've gotta be on the road straight after I drop Maggie at school in the morning."

"I guess," Rosie sighed, suddenly bone tired. "Night."

"Night, love," Declan replied, as they both snuggled down under the covers.

"Mom?"

The small, quiet voice permeated Rosie's sleepy thoughts, making her frown slightly. She tried to pull herself back to reality, but she was really cozy. "Mmm?"

Maggie sounded hesitant, as though she had come into her mom's room as a last resort. "Have you seen my library book?"

Rosie's eyes snapped open, and she twisted her neck trying to simultaneously lean up to peer over Declan at the clock on the bedside table. "Ow!" she yelped, clapping a hand to her instantly-aching neck as she began to drag herself out of bed.

"Shoot," she hissed to herself. "Have you checked

inside your school bag?" she asked Maggie, who was shifting from one foot to the other in the doorway.

"I'll go look," Maggie promised, vanishing.

"Babe, wake up," Rosie said, one hand on Declan's freckled shoulder as she tried to shake him awake.

"Huh?" he grunted, squinting at her.

"We overslept."

"Fuck sake," he groaned, throwing back the covers.

The whole cottage was still a shambles from birthday party and store opening preparation the day before. By the time they arrived home last night no one was in the mood to tidy up.

Gabriel was awake and sitting at the kitchen counter, his cell phone in his hand. It was one of the really expensive ones with all the bells and whistles, and Rosie didn't have to be a witch to be able to foresee that Maggie was going to be jealous and nagging about getting one herself before dinnertime rolled around. She held back a preemptive sigh.

"Good morning, Gabriel," she said, mustering as much pep as she could manage while heading straight to the coffee machine.

"Just Gabe," he corrected her, a little sullenly. "Morning." His accent was freshly-pressed British—posh, not country—and sounded so different to the easy-going conventions of Declan's accent that for a moment it threw Rosie.

She recovered, moving to set out two cups while the coffee percolated. "You sleep okay?"

"Alright," Gabriel said, his eyes never leaving his phone. "Considering it was like sleeping on a sack full of sawdust."

Rosie's hand slipped with the sugar, and she dumped a little too much into her own cup. No one else had complained that the couch was uncomfortable. Had Declan and Tammy endured sleepless nights? The uneasy feeling in her stomach rose to a new level.

"Sorry to hear it," she said genuinely, even if Gabe's approach was a little out of line. "We have an air mattress, if you think that'd be better?"

Gabe shrugged as he continued watching a video silently on his phone. In his free hand he flicked open his lighter. The flame sprang to life and flickered for a few moments before he snapped it shut. "Whatever," he shrugged. "I won't be here long anyway. Once those papers are signed, I'm outta here."

Rosie pursed her lips. She wasn't about to get into that conversation. Taking a quick breath to regroup, she grabbed the cream from the fridge and changed the subject as smoothly as she could.

"We don't usually have time to sit down for a formal breakfast during the week," she told him, forcing an apologetic smile onto her face. "So it's usually cereal—which is in the pantry, or toast—which is in the bread-bin by the toaster." She made her way back to her coffee prep. "I'm going to have some toast. Would you like me make some for you, too?"

"I'm good thanks," he replied calmly, scrolling

through his feed. And then he reached for a candy bar that was in a bowl of other stuff leftover from Maggie's party the day before. Rosie's brows shot upwards as she watched him unwrap it and take a huge bite.

Maggie chose that moment to reemerge, ready for school with her library book held over her head in triumph. She stopped when she saw Gabe, her eyes lighting up.

"Can *I* have candy for breakfast too?" she asked excitedly.

"No," Rosie said, desperately trying not to snap. Declan came in to claim his coffee.

"Why not? *Gabe's* eating some!" Maggie pouted. "No fair!"

"Just put it in your lunch box and eat it at school," Gabe said, his mouth full. "Not like they can't stop you then."

Rosie put down her own cup as she caught Declan's eye across the kitchen. He glanced at Rosie, then at Gabe.

"Yes we can," he interjected, leaning against the kitchen counter with an extra dose of bravado in his usual swagger. "The Irish have the fairies on our side. Our spies are everywhere." He nodded matter-of-factly, before taking a huge gulp of coffee.

Inwardly, Rosie groaned. She wasn't sure that Maggie was going to buy into fairy-spies. Declan might be okay with his kid eating candy for breakfast and setting a bad example, but she didn't have to let hers follow suit. She drew herself up and focused her attention on Maggie instead.

"If you eat candy for breakfast, you'll get a sugar rush and crash out in a couple hours. Then you won't be able to concentrate in class. And," Rosie added, warming to her subject, "it's bad for your teeth. So it's not a great idea, even if you don't get caught doing it."

"And if it's bad for your teeth, then they'll fall out," Gabe advised sagely, which was enough for Rosie to do a double take, until he followed it up with a wily grin. "Therefore the more you eat, the more often the *tooth* fairy will come." He smirked at Rosie. "So the *molar* of the story is—eat more candy!"

Maggie giggled, until she caught the unimpressed look on Rosie's face.

Gabe snorted, slipping off his stool. He dumped his candy wrapper in the trash as he passed on his way to the living room, a jaunty peace sign in the air as he went. Rosie pressed her lips into a thin line and turned to fix Declan with a look that said they would discuss that particular exchange later—in private—before she turned her attention back to Maggie.

"You know where the bread is," she said, sticking to her guns. "Why don't you make yourself some peanut butter on toast?"

Rosie grabbed her coffee, ducking into the bedroom to get herself ready for her day. She pulled on her jeans and a black t-shirt with a band logo on it that she could switch out for her Go-Go Mart polo that afternoon and scooped her hair up into her signature ponytail before emerging to commandeer Fox Cottage's tiny bathroom.

Gabe was laid on the couch, game controller in hand. She raised a brow, stepping into the doorway.

"Hey Gabe?" she said, speaking over the top of the video game. "You're going to work with Declan today, so it'd be a good idea to start getting ready to go."

"What?" Gabe baulked, pausing his game and half sitting up. "I stay home alone at my grandparents' house *all the time*," he argued, "and they have *way* more expensive stuff than you."

Rosie blinked, the insult settling into her already frayed nerves. "All the same," she shot back, keeping her tone level, "in this house it's *my* rules—and I don't allow kids to stay home alone until I know them well enough to know they can be responsible about it."

Declan was shuffling past in his socks, presumably on his way to fetch his work boots. "What's up?" he asked, a worried note in his voice.

"She said I have to go with you to work like a little kid and be bored out of my skull," Gabe sighed.

Declan pursed his lips, lifting a hand to scratch his beard thoughtfully. "Well, there won't be much of anythin' for him to do while I make my deliveries," he pointed out, eliciting a grin from Gabriel. "Maybe it's not a bad idea to let him stay home. At least here he can—"

"He's still a kid, and kids need supervision," Rosie interrupted him. An uneasy feeling had taken up residence in the pit of her stomach, pushing out feeling fingers to see how big it could grow. "Besides. We all only just met him yesterday, and now we're all gonna abandon him for the day?"

"He's old enough to be here on his own," Declan said with a dismissive gesture. "I'm sure it'll be fine."

She paused. She didn't want to straight-up admit that she wasn't comfortable with Gabe staying in the house on his own, but she wasn't about to give in either. Whether Declan liked it or not, his son was his responsibility.

"I'm *not* sure," Rosie told him, a hard edge to her tone. "So, can you please just take him with you like we talked about?"

"Sure," Declan said, his usually lilting accent sounding clipped. He continued into the bedroom, leaving Rosie and Gabriel in his wake. Gabriel smirked before picking up his controller to turn off his video game. Rosie frowned at his back. He was awfully smug for a kid who hadn't gotten their own way.

Ten minutes later, they were all squeezed into Declan's truck and heading down The Ridge into town. The silence was almost as thick as the tension-filled air as the truck rattled and bumped along the road. Declan kept his eyes front and center while Gabe sat next to his father and looked resolutely out of the driver's side window. Maggie was sitting next to the passenger window with her face almost pressed up against the glass, which left Rosie feeling like the piggy in the middle. On instinct, she angled her body towards Maggie's and looked out the passenger window over the top of her daughter's head.

Maggie flung open the door with relief as they got to her school, and she paused just long enough to kiss her mother's cheek and mutter a 'Bye,' to Declan and Gabe. It was unlike Maggie not to thank Declan for the ride, but given the morning had been anything but usual (and seeing how Declan had been unwilling to chastise his own kid for poor manners), Rosie was willing to let it slide just this once. Rosie shuffled over as soon as she could so that she wouldn't have to stay smushed up to Gabe, her hand resting on the door handle in anticipation.

It was a mercifully short drive down Main Street and into the alley that housed Nourish, the shop that Rosie ran with Tammy—her best friend and Mosswood's answer to Martha Stewart. The store itself had once been a hunting shop owned by Tammy's unwholesome ex-husband, but with some paint, some elbow grease, and a lick of magic the place had been transformed into an adorable little cafe, with crafts, preserves, house plants and candy sales. The grand opening just the day before might have been overshadowed by the unexpected arrival of Gabriel, but today was going to be business as usual and Rosie couldn't wait to get started.

The truck rumbled to a halt outside the store, and Rosie flung open the door.

"Good luck today," Declan said to her softly. She

glanced up, her eyes meeting his, and she was momentarily warmed by the genuine kindness she found there. A pang of guilt shot through her, and she opened her mouth to say something back when Gabe cut her off.

"Yeah," he said his voice unusually buoyant. "Good luck—have an absolutely *marvelous* day!"

What the actual fuck?

Rosie blinked behind her sunglasses but recovered as quickly as she could.

"Thanks," she replied warily. "You too, Gabe." She turned with a wave towards Nourish. She hoped she imagined the unmistakable sensation of eyes prickling on the back of her neck as she slipped the key into the lock, opening her store for the first time.

CHAPTER TWO

T he place was already spotless, and not for the first time Rosie found herself thanking the lucky star that saw her become friends with a woman like Tammy. There was no trace of yesterday's party, save for some leftover food that had been carefully stored in the glass refrigerator by the cash register, presumably for today's lunch specials. Rosie let some of the tension escape from her bunched up shoulders and switched on the cute vintage-style radio that sat on a shelf above the milkshake fixings.

Music was such a balm. It wasn't just the notes and lyrics that affected Rosie; her focus on a song gave her mind permission to rest beneath the weight of her troubles. She unstacked the dishes that had been put on to wash before Tammy had closed the afternoon before and then made sure the milk fridge beneath the coffee machine was fully stocked ready for what they were both hoping would be a busy day.

A flash of movement past the tiny window right next to the coffee machine—designed to open for people to place their takeaway coffee orders—made Rosie look up. Tammy hurried to the door of the store, clicked the handle experimentally to see if it was open, and then hurtled herself inside as though she couldn't wait to start her day. The door clattered open recklessly. Plump, kind-faced Tammy was flushed bright red, as though she had sprinted down to Nourish from her beautiful home on Mosswood's most affluent street.

"Tammy?" Rosie said, stepping up to attention as she half greeted and half questioned her friend. "What on *earth*—are you alright?"

"All my *days!*" Tammy gushed, her eyes shining with happiness. "Myles and I are gettin' hitched!" She punched the air with her left hand and said the last word in a pitch that was probably higher than even dogs could hear. Her grin stretched from ear to ear and framed with pretty pink lipstick, and something very sparkly glittered on the ring finger she was waving ecstatically above her head like a victory banner.

"What?!" Rosie screeched excitedly. She began to rush around the counter to her friend, but Tammy couldn't wait and scurried to meet her halfway. They clasped hands and Tammy did a little dance of excitement.

"I *know!*" she squealed, squeezing Rosie's hands with enthusiasm.

Rosie's own troubles were temporarily forgotten in favor of celebrating such happy news. "Oh my," she beamed, squeezing Tammy's hands right back. "Okay— wait. Let's sit down. Tell me everything—with details!"

The pair of them quickly took up residence on the couch by the register that was quickly becoming their unofficial meeting space. Tammy was flapping her left hand in front of her face rapidly as though the weight of her new diamond might somehow help her to calm down. Rosie reached out and caught hold, holding the hand still so she could admire the ring. A pale peach-toned diamond was nestled in an exquisite rose gold Art Deco setting, surrounded with tiny white diamonds. Rosie whistled, angling the ring this way and that to admire the splendor before looking her friend directly in the eye.

"It's the prettiest ring I've ever seen," she said truth-fully, her heart fit to burst. "Now spill the tea."

Tammy grinned and took a breath, like an opera singer preparing for a particularly difficult aria.

"Well," she exhaled excitedly. "We'd had dinner at Minetti's and had gone out for our evening walk, which we try to do most nights. We were down by the river, and we stopped at the lookout to enjoy the view of the falls."

"Awwww!" Rosie sighed happily. The lookout, a large rotunda extending over the water of the river, was one of the most beautiful features of Mosswood. It sounded like such a beautifully contrived location, and she made a mental note to congratulate Myles for his excellent planning. "He's *such* a sweetheart!"

"I *know!*" Tammy agreed, pressing her left hand to her chest as though she was hardly able to believe it herself. "We were standing there, looking out at the water. The moonlight looked just like mercury settled on top of the current. I was talkin' about how pretty it made the dark woods across the river look, and when I turned back to Myles, he was down on one knee!"

"That's *amazing,* Tammy," Rosie cooed, standing up so that she could go and hug her friend. "I'm so happy for you both. Congratulations!"

"Thank you," Tammy beamed, fiddling with her ring. "I *had* been hopin' Myles would pop the question. Made me worry a little about how strange it would feel to wear a ring again, truth be told." She glanced down at the gorgeous engagement ring and for a moment almost seemed lost for words. "But it's been just fine, really. *More* than fine." There were tears shining in her eyes and she looked back up at Rosie, who smiled and changed the course of the conversation to preserve Tammy's mood.

"So!" Rosie asked, her tone suddenly business-like. "What are you guys thinking in terms of the actual wedding?"

It was the first time Tammy had hesitated since swanning into the building. "That's a little more complicated, and a lot less romantic," she said, with a little sigh that raised a red flag for Rosie.

"Why?" she asked warily.

"We just don't wanna rush things, is all," Tammy said. Her attention was suddenly on her manicure, and not on the excitement of her brand-new engagement. "Myles and I are both divorced so we *should* be able to do what we like," she added lightly, "but you know Mosswood. We're just worried that people won't take so kindly to the Pastor movin' on to a new lady so soon. And Prissy cryin' 'poor me!' all over town sure ain't helpin' any."

"Fuck Prissy," Rosie snapped.

"Language!" Tammy blinked, though she knew better than to think her admonishment would get far with Rosie.

Rosie shrugged. "Seriously! I mean it. She hasn't got a say in this. She lost a good man *and* a bad one, and that's on her. Let her feel sorry for herself if she wants, but *don't* let her have any influence on what date you set for your own wedding!"

Their eyes met, and Rosie watched the uncertainty melt from Tammy's gaze.

"You know what?" she asked, starting to look more like the confident, determined woman Rosie had come to know and adore. "You're right! And we don't really *want* to wait, truth be told! Myles goes to a seminary at the end of every summer, and summer's the only time the church isn't already booked solid, on account of there's no air conditioning. So if we don't want to wait until next year then we might just have to rush." She looked a bit sheepishly at Rosie. "We just hate to be the talk of the town for the wrong reasons if we can help it."

"I hate to say it, but people are going to talk regardless," Rosie pointed out, earning herself a nod from Tammy. "If you two wanna get married, then *go* for it!" Rosie sat back, her smile more matter-of-fact. "Life's too damn short to wait on happiness," she said.

A heartbeat later, and Tammy was back in her Ecstatic Fiancé mode. "I think we will! How exciting," she trilled. "Will you be my maid of honor, Rosie? I know Myles plans to ask Ben to be his best man.

"He does?" Rosie asked, surprised that it wasn't Matthew, his son. She recovered in the nick of time. "Of course I'll be your maid of honor! Thank you so much for askin' me!"

"Wonderful!" Tammy exclaimed, sitting back. She looked like the cat that got the cream, full on happiness until something decidedly unhappy started to dawn on her. Her face fell, and she leaned forward empathetically.

"Shoot, I'm so sorry, Rosie," she apologized. "Listen to me, busting in here like a charging bull without even stopping to ask about you." She winced a little as she asked the question Rosie didn't know she had been dreading. "How did everything go with Declan and..." She lowered her tone to a whisper, as though the walls had ears and they were judgmental ones. "His son?"

"Oh, you know," she began, that same uncomfortable feeling rising up in her throat like bile. She was suddenly afraid that if she starting bringing up her worries about Gabe and Declan and what it all meant for their family, she wouldn't be able to stop. She glanced at Tammy's sweet, expectant face and shrugged with as much confidence as she could muster.

"He's settling in," she said in the end. "Gabriel, that is."

"What a lovely religious name!" Tammy breathed, ready to view everything in the world through her rose-colored glasses. And because her friend was the person most deserving of happiness, Rosie was willing to let her.

"I'm sure that once he settles in and gets used to being part of the family he'll fit right in," Tammy promised. "Kids are so wonderful. I just adore Matthew. He's such an intelligent, well-mannered young man. But that doesn't mean I don't secretly hope Myles and I will have some children of our own. Can you imagine?"

Rosie didn't like to point out that Matthew had also egged Rosie and Maggie when they had first arrived in town. She wasn't sure how well-mannered that made him, but she wasn't about to burst Tammy's bubble.

"I've seen you with Maggie," she said instead, pushing her misgivings about Gabe back into the pit of her stomach. "So I don't have to *imagine*. You'll be an amazing mom one day, Tammy."

THE REST OF THE MORNING PASSED IN A BLUR OF serving customers—her own customers in her own store. Rosie drew no small amount of satisfaction from talking to a lady about the best house plant for her kitchen window and telling anyone who wanted something to nibble about Tammy's incredible culinary creations. By the time the lunch crowd had dispersed she was convinced that their second day had been every bit as successful as the first, without the added drama of the day before.

"I'll see you tomorrow afternoon," Rosie called to Tammy as she headed for the door. "Bye, future Mrs. Bishop!"

Tammy grinned behind the counter. "Go on now," she giggled. "Don't want Ben complainin' you're late!"

The grin that comment brought to Rosie vanished not three yards from Nourish's freshly painted front door. A group of teens were leaning against the wall in the laneway that led down to the Go-Go Mart, talking and laughing amongst themselves. At least one of them was smoking, and someone else was playing profanity-filled music from a phone in their pocket. She didn't need to be up close and personal to notice that Gabe was among them.

Rosie could already feel her blood pressure rising and she fought hard to get it under wraps as she marched along the lane towards them. One of the kids noticed her approach and cleared his throat, giving the boy who was smoking time to throw his cigarette onto the ground and cover it with his foot. Rosie raised an eyebrow as she came to a halt not far away. The boy couldn't have been more than thirteen, by the look of him. But he wasn't her concern.

She turned her attention to Gabe.

"Why aren't you with Declan?" she asked, cutting straight to the chase.

Gabe smirked and shrugged in a way that Rosie supposed was meant to make him look cool. "It was boring, so I bailed."

A chuckle went up from someone else in the group until Rosie looked past Gabe. Silence ensued, and the kids just turned their backs and moved a little further along the alley, as though Rosie's uncool parental-type influence couldn't taint them there. She looked back at Gabe.

"You *bailed?*"

Her temper bubbled higher and higher with each passing moment. Declan was supposed to be watching Gabe, and somehow he just hadn't noticed that his brand-new teenage son was missing from his truck?

"That's what I said," Gabe told her with a smirk, glancing at a person who passed right by her from behind. "Hey, man."

Matthew Bishop joined Gabe, glancing back over his shoulder at Rosie. His brows were high on his forehead, and his mouth hinted at a sarcastic smile just beneath the thin veneer of the 'manners' Tammy had mentioned.

"Good afternoon, Mrs. Bell," he drawled. His features were more like his mother's than his father's, and Rosie couldn't help but think it was a pity. "We were all just headin' down to Granny's for milkshakes." He looked pointedly at her uniform, and then grinned insolently. "Care to join us?"

Ugh. Rosie resisted the urge to glare at him... but only just. She really wanted to give Gabe a chance, but his behavior so far and the fact that he had somehow already formed a bond with the most unpleasant kid in town was making it impossible for her to be charitable.

"No thanks," she replied, tucking her hands into her pockets in case she was tempted to reach and strangle one—or both—of them.

"That's a real shame," Matthew tutted. "I hear they're understaffed."

Another spurt of laughter erupted from the group. Rosie rolled her eyes and her response flew out of her before she could rein it in.

"Good! Maybe you can get a job so the entire congregation of Mosswood isn't crowdfunding your big boy drawers."

Matthew froze. Gabe snorted beside him, and another nearby teen guffawed. "Is that what you bought with my tithe last week?" he asked, pushing Matthew in the shoulder.

At the murderous look on Matthew's face, Rosie regretted saying anything at all. There really was no excuse for grown people tearing down children, even children who were as nasty as Matthew Bishop. Besides, she had been teased over money growing up and she wouldn't wish it on anyone—even if Matthew would be teased for *having* money where she had been teased for *not*.

"Gabriel," she said in the hopes of letting the contention between herself and Matthew die down. "Why don't you get back to Fox Cottage and Declan can meet you there?"

She specifically avoided the word 'home' but Gabriel's sneer made her feel her care was ill-placed.

"I don't think I will, thanks." He met Rosie's eyes defiantly.

She took a breath. "Okay," she said slowly. With Herculean effort she tried to channel the patient tone she used with Maggie, though with another person's child it was slower in coming to her. "But I hope you'll be smart while you're out and be home in time for dinner."

She heard the word as soon as it left her mouth and winced when she was done speaking. It didn't seem to dissuade Gabriel, whose smirk didn't reach his eyes.

"It's not my home, though, is it?"

The two of them stared at each other, gazes locked. He viewed her as the enemy, but she knew he'd say something like that because she had said it growing up, too. So how big a divide could there be?

"Not yet, maybe," she said at last. She walked past the other teens without a glance at them. When she got to the steel ladder set into the wall that would let her up onto the loading dock of the Go-Go she hoisted herself up and disappeared inside.

She chewed the inside of her cheek thoughtfully as she stowed her purse. It wasn't like she could go and speak to Myles or Tammy about Matthew without ruining their engagement buzz and tackling Gabe would have to wait until she got home after work at any rate. Declan was her last resort, and if he was as willing to let Gabe off the hook as he seemed then it didn't bode well for family relations at Fox Cottage.

Rosie waited outside the Go-Go Mart after her shift for a full fifteen irritated minutes until she realized that Declan wasn't coming to pick her up. She hefted her purse and resolutely set off down Main Street, her stomach heavy with worry. It wasn't like him to forget her. She walked home in the later afternoon sunshine as quickly as she could, her imagination twisting itself in knots. God, maybe he'd had an accident? Maybe the truck had broken down...

But he hadn't, and it hadn't. As she rounded the bend in the access road that afforded the first view of

Fox Cottage she could see it was parked squarely on the lawn of Fox Cottage, in its usual place.

Relief momentarily flooded her, until she heard what sounded like military combat as she stomped up the drive. The rattle of machine guns was almost deafening as she shoved open the front door and then gasped.

Declan and Gabe were sitting on dining chairs in the living room, each of them holding a gaming controller and looking up at the brand new flatscreen TV that was dominating the living room wall. They were playing some kind of black ops game on a console she had never seen before.

"No!" Declan yelled, struggling to be heard over the TV volume. "Bah. Head 'round back and we'll rendezvous at the—" he glanced at Rosie's movement over his shoulder an immediately faltered. "Shit," he hissed, setting down the controller. "Sorry, love. I forgot—"

"Where did all this come from?" Rosie asked flatly. She felt her chest constricting with familiar tightness as she mentally tallied up how much the new set-up must have cost.

"I brought it in my luggage," Gabe grinned, continuing to blast online opponents even though Declan clearly wasn't ready.

"The console is Gabe's," Declan clarified, "and the TV is ours. I bought it today. It's a smart TV, so I also got us hooked up for an internet connection. You don't like it?"

She really *didn't* like it. The small second-hand television that had been in the house when they arrived had seemed to suit the feeling of Fox Cottage. It wasn't much of a distraction for Maggie, who was so turned off by how old the TV was that she preferred a book—or, now, the iPad the grownups in her life had jointly gifted to her for her birthday. Rosie wasn't much tempted by the old TV either, so it held its proper place as something to be specifically planned to enjoy rather than a vortex of time-eating brainlessness where people defaulted without thinking.

This new monstrosity commanded the entire wall above the fireplace, even *larger* than the fireplace, and in her mind the entire feeling of the room changed with its presence. And not *just* because the sounds of warfare greeted her at the door.

"No, I don't," she decided to be honest. "Which you would have known if you had consulted me before buying it, like we agreed we would before any big purchases."

"They're going to kick you from the match," Gabriel interrupted. Declan's gaze swung from Rosie to the teen and then back again.

"I'm going to go get changed," Rosie said. Her shoulders sank a little lower than she normally held them. "We have Maggie's middle school thing to go to."

She turned into the bedroom. Closing the door behind her did very little to block out the terrible sounds of their game, but it went a long way towards getting her a little temporary solitude. She wouldn't have time to shower, thanks to the time she had wasted waiting on Declan to pick her up. She kicked off her shoes and slipped out of her Go-Go Mart uniform before pausing to drag a brush through her bedraggled hair.

The quiet click of the bedroom door closing behind her was enough to make her feel tense all over again. She wasn't ready to have this conversation with Declan —and they had to be back at the school in less than half an hour—but she couldn't see how she could avoid it now, either. She chose to say nothing for the moment, brushing her hair until she felt one of Declan's warm hands curve around the front of her waist as he came to stand behind her. She turned, taking a step back to put a little distance between them as she crossed her arms over her chest.

"What the *hell,* Declan?" She frowned up into his face. "I waited at work for you for *fifteen minutes* before I realized you weren't coming, and then spent the whole walk home imagining all the terrible things that must have happened to you! And then I walk in to find out that you're fine—you were just playing stupid video games on a giant TV that I didn't know a damn thing about!"

He hesitated, clearly having underestimated the depth of his own stupidity. After a moment, his shoulders sagged. "You're right," he said, "I'm really sorry darlin'." He reached up to pinch the bridge of his nose, as though it might somehow provide him with more clarity.

Rosie raised a brow. "Why the TV?" she asked, continuing to brush her hair before scooping it back up into a neat ponytail.

"It was on sale," he said, as though hoping it might lessen the trouble he was in. "Gabe told me about his game console, and that he couldn't play it on the old TV. I thought it was something he could do during the summer when we're all busy. An' I've got a lot of birthdays and Christmases and Just Becauses to be makin' up for," Declan confessed, giving a half-shrug and gesturing with his hand. "I thought it might keep him out of trouble."

Rosie huffed a humorless laugh through her nose and shook her head. "You mean like hanging out with a pack of teenagers in the lane when he was supposed to be at work with you today?"

Declan paled. "That little..." He exhaled heavily. "We were on our way back from Rome and he told me he was feelin' car-sick and said he wanted to lie down, so I dropped him off here." His face fell and he looked down at the floorboards in the bedroom, the reality of being duped by a wily teen sinking in.

Thinking back to Maggie doing magic live on YouTube in her room, Rosie softened. He wasn't the only person to have ever had the wool pulled over their eyes by their kid.

"I know you're brand new to being a Dad," she told

him, getting changed as they talked, "but you have *got* to wise up! You *knew* this morning that he didn't want to go with you, and you fell for the first trick he had up his sleeve. And then you *rewarded* him for it with a new TV?"

"Ugh," he groaned, letting his head fall back before he raked his fingers through his wild red hair. "You're right—again. I'm an eejit!"

"A little," she agreed lightly, giving him a sassy 'yeah, I said it' look when he glanced at her. "But you're not the first, and you won't be the last where raising kids is concerned."

He sighed, tugging his shirt over his head so that he could get changed, too. "Good to know."

"What *would* be good to know is if you're thinking about making permanent changes to something in my house or if you can't make it to collect me from work when you promised you would," Rosie pointed out.

"I'm really sorry, love," he said, and this time she allowed him to slide in closer for a cuddle. That same strange uneasiness she had been feeling since Gabe had walked into their lives the day before grew like a weed, tangling itself up inside of her. Suddenly even their usual day-to-day considerations seemed to have taken a back seat to Gabriel in Declan's mind. Her inner Rosie shook her head, determined not to let the uncertainty she was feeing get a foothold.

One thing at a time.

"You stay here with Gabe," she said. "I'll take

Maggie to the parent night. We'll just do our best while we're figuring things out."

"Don't be silly," he murmured as she opened the bedroom door. "I *want* to go with you and Maggie to the parent night."

Rosie paused in the living room hallway, relief flooding through her. "Thank *goodness*," she sighed with a half-smile. "Because I did *not* want to have to face the fact that my baby is heading into middle school alone."

Declan followed her, a reassuring smile on his face. "You won't be," he promised. He reached down to cup her face with his hand and plant a quick but affectionate kiss on her lips.

Rosie leaned into the kiss with her eyes closed, opening them as they pulled away from each other to see Gabe sitting on the couch watching them. His game was running in the background but he was focused on Rosie and Declan instead, brows drawn together in consternation and his head tilted slightly to one side so that his blonde shaggy locks obscured less of his face.

Maggie was ready for once, and presented herself in the hallway, arms held up as though she were Julius Caesar entering Egypt. Her enthusiasm in dressing herself 'appropriately' could be seen in the care she'd taken in selecting a navy-blue top to go with her jeans instead of her rainbow one, and in wearing flats instead of her beat-up school sneakers.

"How do I look?" she asked with a dramatic twirl.

"Very grown up," Declan told her, which earned him a wide grin from Maggie.

Gabe glanced from Rosie to Maggie, his face twisting into a sneer. His attention shifted to Declan and he snorted with derision, reaching for his glass of water on the side table before turning back to his game.

Rosie reached for her purse, hanging on its usual hook by the door. "Gabe, we're leaving."

"Ciao," he said without moving.

Rosie cocked her head to one side involuntarily. Her eyebrows climbed her forehead as though scurrying for cover. "You can't stay here alone."

"I'm not going to some stupid baby school thing," Gabe declared, unleashing a new round of machine-gun fire at his virtual opponents.

Rosie's head swung back upright as she rose to her full height. She had just opened her mouth to respond when Declan shifted uncomfortably next to her.

"Sorry love," he began hesitantly. "I already told him earlier that he didn't need to come tonight."

Rosie swung on her boyfriend in disbelief, her head tilted again in the other direction as though physically swinging from one afront to another. "You neglected to mention that before now," she said icily.

"It'll be grand," Declan said, trying to convince her. "Don't be worryin' about it, Rosie. It'll be boring for him anyway."

"Yeah, Rosie," Gabriel agreed triumphantly. He

picked up his controller again and pressed a center button. "It'll be grand."

"We're gonna be late," Declan added as he passed her for the door, and Rosie felt the situation totally get away from her. She stood taller, hoping to command the attention of both Y chromosomes.

"Lock the doors," she ordered, "Don't go outside. Our numbers are on the fridge if you need anything."

She took a breath, her brain scrolling through a hundred other things that she might need to tell him. Did they have anything for him to eat if he got hungry? Did she need to lockup or hide anything, if he was the sort of kid who would steal credit cards to book a plane flight to America? If he did disobey and go outside for some reason, did he know what to do if he encountered a black bear or a coyote?

The sound of the screen door swinging shut behind Declan tolled the death knoll for any further instructions. She shook her head and gestured again.

"We'll be back in a couple of hours," she announced as she followed after him.

As the three of them piled into the truck and Declan turned on the ignition, Rosie watched the light from the huge television in the living room spill bloody gunpowder colors through the stained-glass window, and she tried not to think about the amount of damage one very stubborn and angry young man could do unsupervised.

CHAPTER THREE

Rosie's brain felt like an over-filled balloon ready to pop. After the meeting at Maggie's new school sample schedules, school policies and other information pressed against the inside of her skull. Declan quietly kept both hands on the steering wheel, his serious expression partly obscured by the darkness. Maggie's constant stream of excited chatter kept her from dwelling too much on whether he was brooding or just overwhelmed like she was.

"It's gonna be so *cool* to have my own locker," Maggie gushed. "And different teachers for everything instead of just one! And *no uniform!*"

"So cool," Rosie agreed absently, peering out of the windshield in the direction of Fox Cottage. She couldn't see the actual house for the trees, but it looked as though every light in the place was on. She sucked in a deep breath. Their electricity bill for the month was going to skyrocket. She was mentally tallying the damages of a doubled electric bill when they rounded the bend that opened into their driveway and Declan hit the brakes.

Rosie gasped.

A pair of teenagers jumped at the sudden arrival of the truck that had almost hit them, squinting into the headlights before raising arms to shield their eyes. Each of them held a red solo cup that they were obviously trying not to spill as they scurried off the driveway and onto the lawn. Rosie watched them go, her mouth open in surprise. She might have questioned her sanity, had it not been for the fact that Declan had stopped the truck so suddenly.

"Check it out," Maggie said, wriggling to the front of the seat so that she could see better.

Cars were lined along the drive and parked everywhere across the front lawn of Fox Cottage, haphazardly pulled in as though the valet had taken an indefinite vacation. People drifted among them, shuffling along with arms draped around friends laughing and shouting to one another across the expanse. The grass itself was littered with even more cups that hinted at several drunk 'someones' in the nearby vicinity.

Declan pulled the truck into the drive so that it was squarely blocking off access to the property and cut the engine. Rosie got out of the truck, looking around as she waited for Maggie to scramble down. The sound of music thumping from the direction of the clearing in the woods sent a shiver up Rosie's spine. She turned her gaze in that direction, noticing the orange glow on the tips of the trees.

Fire.

She started in that direction before her common sense could stop her, with Maggie and Declan on her heels. She could see the flames through the trees as she ran. Pushing herself harder Rosie made it to the clearing in record time, out of breath and high on adrenaline. She skidded to a halt as she made it out into the long grass, gasping for breath that was flavored with woodsmoke.

A huge bonfire had been lit in the middle of the clearing, only just shy of the long grass that filled the whole space this time of year. It wasn't a forest fire like she had originally feared—but only because none of the flying sparks had yet caught the aging piles of wild pine needles from the trees nearby.

A crowd was gathered around the fire. They must have invited every teenager In the county to get a gathering this big. Someone had managed to get their truck all the way up there, which was the source of the throbbing music. Laughter rang out from one cluster of people in the group, as though someone had just told a joke. Rosie's gaze homed in on them, her eyes narrowing when she spotted Gabe's unruly blonde hair in the crowd.

She was already furious when she began marching through the people partying, but her anger reached new heights when she noticed that Gabe was standing right next to Matthew Freakin' Bishop.

As though she could feel Rosie's rage like an electrical current, Maggie stepped behind her mother. Declan stopped by her side, his eyes wide and his jaw set as though he was trying to hold in a few choice expletives.

"What's going *on* here?" Rosie demanded, raising her voice so she could be heard above the music.

Gabe looked her over lazily, as though sizing her up. She held her ground as his mossy gaze reached her eyes, her brows lifting by way of a silent challenge. Matthew turned his head away and said something out of the side of his mouth to Gabe. From the answering boost to Gabe's smug grin, she guessed that it hadn't been concern for their situation.

Gabe gestured to Maggie with the hand that was holding a drink.

"Just doing our part to prepare Maggie for becoming a teenager," he said. He leaned down and held his cup out to Maggie. "Drink up, kid!"

The teens in the immediate vicinity laughed, and then 'ooohed' as Rosie furiously slapped the cup out of Gabe's hand. Maggie jumped and Declan started to move as though he was ready to intervene, but then stopped himself.

"Hey!" Gabe protested, looking at his cup in the grass and then glaring at Rosie. But she was beyond caring about Gabe's hurt feelings or treading lightly around the new arrival.

"Hand my baby poison again and you'll lose much

more than that," she said, deadly serious. Gabe's face paled a little, but when some of the other teens laughed and ahhhed, he glanced around and joined in.

She didn't bother to wait and see how Declan would deal with this new hurdle in his tentative foray into parenthood. She wheeled around, one arm shooting out to curl protectively around Maggie's shoulders as she drew her child away from the party.

"Shut it down," she growled at Declan as she walked past, heading for the cottage.

ROSIE WAS STILL SEETHING WHEN THE BEDROOM DOOR opened a while later. Her best plans—to tell Declan to pull it together and to point out that Gabe was already causing the kind of trouble that would get out of hand really fast if he didn't step in and do something—were swallowed whole by the tension in the darkness.

His huge form sounded clumsy by default. Floorboards creaked beneath his weight, and the door clicked louder than he would have liked as he closed it behind him. She could almost even hear him wince as he desperately tried not to disturb her. He didn't know her as well as he thought, if he thought there was any way she was getting to sleep after an evening like *that*.

Rosie held back a sigh, rolling to sit up in bed and turn on the lamp beside her. Declan froze as light flooded the room, caught in the act of sneaking over to his side of the bed. Once he realized that Rosie was very awake, his broad shoulders sagged in defeat.

Rosie hesitated, but then her desire to know what happened got the best of her. "Well?"

Declan glanced over his shoulder as he perched on the edge of the bed. "Well *what?"* he asked defensively.

All of Rosie's ability to approach this conversation without resorting to 'easy blame' flew right out the window. Her temper was spiked, and her sense of injustice was riled up right along with it. She sat up a little straighter, keeping her voice low because she wouldn't have put it past Gabe to be listening in on the other side of their bedroom door. "Well—what have you got to say for your kid?!" she whispered.

Declan bent to pull his shoes off and then stood again to get undressed.

"He's a *teenager*, Rosie," he sighed, closing his eyes briefly in frustration before levelling a pointed look at her. "I can't baby him the way you do with Maggie!"

Silence reigned in the moments since that shot was fired. Rosie's brows were high on her forehead, and her blood pressure was up there alongside them. She took one deep breath and then another, trying to hold on to her temper as it pawed the ground and struggled to break out of her grip.

"What?" she blinked, locking her teeth together as soon as the word escaped her.

"Oh c'mon," he drawled, looking at Rosie with skepticism. "You *still* tuck her in at night, and hold her hand while ya walkin' with her." He shook his head, holding up a hand in the direction of Maggie's room. "She's goin' on for a teenager, Rosie—it's time you let her grow up a bit!"

"Well Gabe is only fourteen," Rosie snapped back. "Just a few years older than Maggie—not graduating high school like those boys he's hanging out with! And being a teenager is one thing, but deliberately doing things he knows we won't want him doing and then flaunting it in our faces isn't okay!"

"D'ya really think Maggie won't do that later on?" Declan asked, standing and putting his hands on his hips. "I've got one word for ya, Rosie. *Rabbits*."

The bitterness she'd experienced in the Spring with Maggie and the COW and the ever-impending thread of Greybriar Academy came back to haunt her. She was *painfully* aware of her only child's inevitable march into adulthood.

"I don't doubt that she will," she said, crossing her arms over her chest. "But when she does, I'll be *handling* it instead of letting her just do whatever the hell she wants!"

"He's used to a certain amount of freedom," Declan explained, tossing his shirt on the floor and gesturing in the direction of the couch in the next room. "If I suddenly start comin' down on him like a hard-arse, d'ya really think that's gonna get me very far?"

Rosie scoffed in disbelief. "There's a difference between being a hard ass and letting him get away with murder," she pointed out. "He's been rude and deliberately troublesome. He skipped out on hanging out with you at work, then guilted you into buying a television for him, and *then* he chose to skip out supporting Maggie tonight, and you let him! And *now* he's trashed the property by inviting half of Georgia to a bonfire party in the middle of fire season!"

Declan flapped his hands in the air. "So what do you want me to do? Sign the papers? Let him be on his own?"

"I want you to be a parent!" she blurted with exasperation, flapping her hands in a mirror image of his gesture. "Give him ground rules! Give him guidance! He's trying to get you to sign the papers, so don't let him get away with it."

A moment zipped between them, as hot and as dangerous as one of the embers from Gabriel's bonfire.

"I won't sign the papers," Declan declared stubbornly. "Either he stays with me, or I give custody to his grandparents."

Rosie stared, not even daring to breathe because words might come out with the breath. The flare of Declan's nostrils and the set of his jaw told Rosie he meant every word. Gabriel would be a part of Rosie and Maggie's life as long as Declan was. The announcement left her almost as shell-shocked as learning he had a son must have left Declan.

He met her eyes across the bed, and then his shoulders sagged again. "I need your help, Rosie," he said more quietly than he had been speaking before. "I know he's a mess, and I've not got any right to be raisin' a kid. But he's *mine*, and it's my fault he hasn't got a mother anymore and never had a father to begin with."

"No, it isn't," Rosie instantly responded. She stepped forward, placing her hands on his arms to command his attention as she looked up at him. "None of this is your fault. If there is anyone to blame, it's Gemma."

She settled her shoulders and her jaw, taking a deep breath as though that might put her heart back where it was supposed to be. "But you're right. He's our—" She almost called him a 'problem', but thought to correct herself at the last moment. "—Responsibility now. So." She gave a half-shrug and met Declan's gaze. "We'll just have to figure it out."

Declan's shoulders relaxed. "Really?" he asked, eyes skipping back and forth between hers.

She hoped her hesitance was less obvious to him than it was to her. "Absolutely," she said more confidently than she felt. Her eyes landed on the emancipation papers Declan had stashed on the mantle in the bedroom and picked them up, tossing them into the empty fireplace, where they settled into the remnants of ashes in the corners leftover from the spring cleaning. Even though the gesture was symbolic, her heart jumped into her throat.

Declan pulled her into his burly hug, clinging like he never intended to let her go.

CHAPTER FOUR

Weekends were usually quiet, relaxing days at Fox Cottage. Reading, visiting with friends and a spot of gardening were usually the order of the day, with hearty home-cooked meals and maybe an evening board game for kicks. But this was the first weekend in a long time that the cottage had housed four people instead of just three, and after her fight with Declan the night before Rosie was feeling more than a little claustrophobic.

She'd escaped the house to bring the laundry in off the line, but as nice as the weather was she could hardly linger all day behind clean sheets that were already dry. Her feet felt like anchors as she trudged back up to the house, laundry basket on her hip. The kitchen was usually her safe space so she made her way there, only noticing her mistake after she'd deposited her basket onto the counter.

Gabe glanced up at her, his thumb poised in the middle of his never-ending scroll through his news feed. One of his light brows jumped but then sunk, as though his surprise that she was joining him was soon replaced with cynicism after seeing her expression. Rosie gave herself a mental reminder to work on her poker face, reached into her basket and shook out a sheet. The snapping sound that it made heralded silence.

At first Rosie thought that she might prefer it. If he could focus on his phone and she could channel all her energy into folding laundry, they might just get through this forced proximity situation in one piece. But as she folded piece after piece of clean linen and then moved onto t-shirts and other clothes, their unspoken words rumbled like thunder in the distance. She found herself casting glances in Gabe's direction, and in the back of her mind she wished that he would move to literally anywhere else in the house.

And then the tension broke like a storm.

"There's no need, you know." He didn't bother to look up from his phone.

Rosie took a quick breath and a small frown creased her brow, and she glanced at him over the top of her sheet folding before she could stop herself. "No need for what?"

He shrugged. "To feel awkward."

That he hit the nail on the head and had the guts to bring it up in conversation both impressed and mortified her. "I don't feel awkward," she lied, the hint of a breathy laugh in her tone as though the very idea was ridiculous. She folded a pair of Maggie's shorts and took her time tucking them onto the top of her laundry pile.

"Yes you do," Gabe said, his voice quiet enough that it drew Rosie's attention back to him. When she looked over his head was down, his eyes at the floor instead of his phone. He glanced at her furtively, and then back at his phone. "But it's okay. I already know you don't want me here." He skipped a beat before adding, "I'm never wanted anywhere."

Her hands slowed as she folded a dish towel, taking an inordinate amount of time to square up the corners. The accent might have been different—posh English instead of city Southern—but the words and the feeling behind them were all too familiar. She'd said them many times growing up, in various foster homes around the state, in many living rooms, or backyard forts, or on the back of a motorcycle outside of a high school football game. She also remembered the first time she'd ever heard someone say they *did* want her, and the nearly twenty years of unhappiness it had caused. She didn't want the wrong person to be the first person to tell Gabe he was wanted.

"Your father wants you here," she said honestly. She at last placed the dish towel she'd been fiddling with into the basket.

Gabe snorted, a quiet sound that didn't carry the

force it once had. "Thanks, but… I'm young, not stupid."

He stood from the table and seconds later, the front door opened and then closed behind him.

Rosie leaned her hip into the kitchen counter, letting it bear her weight for a moment. It took the pressure off her tired feet, but not off her soul. She sighed, glancing at the laundry basket as though looking for advice. When none came, she decided she better get on with it.

IT WAS ONE OF THOSE PICTURE PERFECT EARLY SUMMER days. Bright blue sky stretched up for an eternity, with a small flock of fluffy white clouds dotted far away on the horizon. A light breeze took any of the bite out of the rising sun, and Rosie found herself feeling more relaxed than she had since the moment Gabe had stumbled into their lives. Her sunglasses helped her define the world below, and she surveyed the picturesque town of Mosswood as the pair of them made their way down The Ridge.

"Can I really make money doing chores for you and Aunt Tammy at Nourish this summer?" Maggie asked, her eager steps carrying her along a good two or three yards ahead of Rosie.

"Yep. And Ben said he could use a little help at the Go Go, too." Rosie smiled proudly, pleased to see Maggie excited about the prospect.

Maggie hi-fived the air. "Neat!"

"You think that now," Rosie laughed, tucking her hands into the pockets of her jeans as they strolled down the slope towards the highway. "But it'll be work— believe me," she added. "I don't think you'll feel it's so neat when you're working instead of hanging out with your friends all the time. But sticking with something tough and makin' it into something you're proud of brings its own rewards."

"Like a cell phone!" Maggie added, grinning.

"Like a cell phone," Rosie agreed. She glanced up and noticed that the Sheriff's police Jeep was pulled up outside the old Hayes Sugar and Syrup Mill on the corner of the access road to the woods and the highway. Her heart kicked up a gear for a moment—residual panic no doubt left over from her dealings with the previous Sheriff, Larry Holt—before she noticed that Mosswood's new Sheriff wasn't alone. The petite blonde woman in khaki was talking to another woman, whose hawkish face and hunched posture made her instantly recognizable to Rosie.

Carol-Ann.

Rosie raised her hand in a wave as they got closer to the pair, receiving two half-hearted acknowledgements for her trouble. Maggie charged on ahead, clearly interested in speaking to one or both of the other women.

"Don't go too far," Rosie called, with a smile that faded when Maggie stopped in her tracks. She was looking at something with her hands clapped dramatically over her mouth, and Rosie followed her line of sight as they neared the corner of the highway where Sheriff Harper Star and Carol-Ann were talking animatedly together, gesturing at the thing that had drawn Maggie's attention.

The 'thing' was a giant penis, spray-painted in bright pink juvenile glory on the side of the Mill building, among many other graffiti that would have made the pastor blush.

Rosie's mouth fell open and her eyes widened in shock. She looked to Maggie, preparing to turn her kid away from such a lurid display. But a snicker escaped the hand that Maggie had clapped to her own mouth, followed by a fully-formed giggle in short order. Rosie frowned, discomfort and embarrassment bubbling in the bottom of her stomach. There was another sensation there, too. Something that Rosie couldn't quite describe...

When did her young daughter start to find things like this funny? And was it time to have *that conversation* with Maggie? She felt like it was too early to be worrying about all this... but a small voice in the back of her mind reminded her that kids were different compared to what it was like when she was growing up.

Sheriff Star huffed with frustration as Rosie and Maggie drew nearer.

"We need to get this removed," she said, glancing in Maggie's direction and then at Rosie apologetically before lowering her voice to Carol-Ann. "*Fast.*"

"I'm not sure what you think *I* can do about removing a ten-foot-tall phallus off a red brick wall," Carol-Ann said, deadpan.

The Sheriff blushed at the use of the word *phallus* and flapped her hands in frustration. "I dunno. *Call* someone?"

Carol-Ann lifted a brow, her hawkish gaze penetrating. "Like *who?*"

"The owner'd be a good start," Sheriff Star said.

"And how am *I* supposed to know who the owner is?" Carol-Ann asked.

"You're tellin' me that *you*—who knows about every damn property in this town," Sheriff Star said suspiciously to Carol-Ann, "aren't even sure who this giant, derelict fire-trap belongs to?"

Carol-Ann was already riled. Rosie could see it from the determined set of the older woman's bony shoulders. She knew enough about Mosswood's resident realtor/business landlord/secret witch's familiar/were-skunk to know that Carol-Ann was rapidly nearing the end of her rope.

"Why *should* I?" she fired back at the Sheriff, glancing at Rosie and Maggie as they approached. "Never been sold, far as I can tell. Ain't never been rented, either. So either it belongs to the county, or the original owners."

"The *original* owners?" Sheriff Star scoffed. "Like, from back in the day?" The Sheriff sighed, digging her keys out of her pocket and heading for her Jeep. "I'll contact the county office first and see what they can tell me."

"Glad to be of service," Carol-Ann murmured wryly, nodding her farewell at the Sheriff as she took off. Maggie's astute gaze flicked between Carol-Ann and her mother, and she wandered over to the corner so that she could see if there were any horses in the fields next to the Vet clinic across the highway.

"You recognize it?" Carol-Ann asked blatantly, making Rosie blink.

"The... *phallus?*" she asked in a hushed, scandalized whisper.

Carol-Ann snorted with genuine amusement, shooting Rosie a look that might as well have said *bless your heart.*

"The *magic* you ninny," Carol-Ann specified, her lips still turned up in a smirk. It hit her like a shot of pink spray-paint to the eyeballs, and Rosie whipped around to look at the huge penis for a second time. Sure enough, she could feel traces of magic etched into the brick wall of the Mill right alongside the paint. As she reached out with her magical energy Rosie could sense anger, defiance, and most of all—uncertainty. She narrowed her eyes as the sound of a truck broke through her revelation.

Maggie had waved at Declan and Gabe as they had pulled off the highway, passing the Sheriff as she headed back into town. But Rosie found herself simply staring at the familiar truck as it approached her and

Carol-Ann. Declan was the closest to her, and Rosie could see that he was caught between wanting to greet her and not knowing what to say. But her eyes skipped past him and settled straight onto Gabe, who was smirking at his handiwork on the side of the building as they passed by.

"I gotta get Maggie to school," Rosie said distract-edly, watching the truck disappear up The Ridge.

"Mmhmm," Carol-Ann hummed, her eyes also trained on the truck as it slipped around a bend and into the woods.

CHAPTER FIVE

R osie stood at the kitchen sink washing dishes
that Friday afternoon when two skinny arms
captured her waist in a hug. She didn't know
how much longer Maggie was going to want impromptu
cuddles, but she was willing to keep them on the menu
for as long as possible. Rosie paused, the dish cloth
mid-swipe, the bond with her daughter evident through
their matching, intermingled magical auras.

"I love you, Mommy," Maggie said, in a small voice
that she was intentionally trying to make sound even
smaller. Cutesy, even.

Rosie raised a brow, glancing over her shoulder to
peer suspiciously at her daughter. "What do you want?"
she asked.

A flicker of guilt at being caught out so quickly
passed across Maggie's face before she shrugged and

smile. "Nothing," she said, squeezing. "I just love you is all."

"I wasn't born yesterday, Magnolia."

Maggie took a breath, releasing her mother. "Would you mind if I don't go with you to Aunt Tammy's?" she asked, grabbing a dish towel and starting to dry the dishes her mom had just washed. "You two are just going to be doing boring wedding planning stuff! I have a bunch of homework to finish, and I really wanna finish my new library book so I can take it back tomorrow."

And so it continued: the push and pull of a child wanting more freedom and the parent 'knowing' that it was a recipe for disaster. Rosie had been learning to let go bit by bit, but they definitely hadn't graduated to Maggie being left home alone for any length of time. The front door opened and closed, signaling Declan and Gabe's arrival home.

"Sorry Pumpkin," Rosie said, continuing with the dishes, "but you're not old enough yet to stay home on your own."

Declan entered the kitchen, making his way straight to the sink. Rosie leaned towards him so that he could plant a peck on her lips, and then he tugged Maggie into a one-armed hug.

"How are my favorite girls?" he asked, his mossy green gaze skipping between them.

Maggie looked between Declan and her mom and then back again, ignoring the fact that Declan's hug made it impossible to keep drying the plate she was holding.

"What about Declan?" she asked hopefully.

He blinked. "What *about* Declan?"

"Can I stay here with you this afternoon instead of going with Mom to Aunt Tammy's for wedding stuff?" Maggie unleashed the full force of her puppy-dog eyes on him. "Pretty please?"

Declan pressed his lips together, his head canting to one side as he threw a quick glance at Rosie. It was the first time Maggie had reached out to him since Gabe had come onto the scene, as though she had sensed the underlying current of the girls vs. boys mentality in the house. A pang of guilt shot through Rosie, but she already knew what his answer was going to be.

"I can't, wee'an," he sighed, reverting to his nickname for her the way a duck finds water. "I've gotta go straight back out to Rome this afternoon to drop off some emergency stock to a customer out there." He fixed her with an apologetic look.

"I could watch her."

A new voice in the equation made all three of them turn to look at Gabriel. He was standing in the open doorway between the kitchen and the living room, one shoulder against the wall. His scruffy hair was tamped down a little, and Rosie wondered whether it was Declan's influence, or the fact that there seemed to be more teenage girls in Mosswood than there did teenage boys.

Maggie brightened visibly, clearly surprised that Gabe would offer to do something so cool for her. "Seriously?"

He shrugged nonchalantly. "I'm not doing anything."

Maggie rounded on Rosie with all the tenacity of a wild animal sensing victory was nigh. "Pleeeeeeease, Mom?"

Rosie's initial gut reaction was a big fat *no way.* Since his arrival, Gabe had done everything possible to prove that he was the least reliable babysitter in a ten-mile radius. Was she really supposed to just up and trust him because he'd used a little hair gel and had offered to take up the post? Rosie tried to keep her doubts from showing on her face, giving Gabe a tight, uncomfortable smile that was a long way off passing for grateful.

"That's very kind of you, Gabe, but I think Maggie would be better off coming with me to Tammy's." Rosie turned to Maggie, whose downtrodden expression wasn't enough to outweigh her mother's apprehension. "You can bring your homework and your book with you."

"Whatever," Gabe said, as though he couldn't have cared less. He disappeared back into the living room, where he had been cozied up with his video game.

"It's not fair," Maggie declared under her breath, heading for her room.

Rosie let out the rest of her breath as the room emptied of people under the age of fifteen, her shoulders sagging as she washed the last two dishes. She was about to dry them when Declan took up the dish towel Maggie had abandoned and did it for her.

"She'll be fine here, love," he suggested lightly. "We'll only be gone a couple of hours."

She lifted an eyebrow at him as though he'd grown another head. "He handed Maggie a beer a little less than a week ago, Declan."

"He apologized for that," Declan added, a note of defensiveness creeping into his tone.

"Did he?" Rosie asked. "Not to me."

Declan put the last dish away and turned to Rosie, his arms slipping around her waist in a grown-up version of Maggie's hug earlier. His energy was filled with uncertainty and longing. She sighed as he spoke gently to her, obviously not wanting the kids to overhear.

"This is a perfect opportunity for them to spend a little bonding time together," he told her. "Things have been so..."

"Strained?" she supplied, quirking a brow at him.

"Yeah," he agreed reluctantly. He flashed her a quick, tight smile that didn't reach his eyes. "It'd be nice for Gabe to look after Maggie a bit. One less thing for us to be worryin' about. What d'ya think?"

Rosie hesitated, searching for a way to say no. She didn't trust Gabe one little bit... but she couldn't hold a grudge against a fourteen-year-old kid. He needed opportunities to do better. But Maggie was still small, and—

You're babying her again, that nagging voice in the back of her mind hearkened back to her argument with Declan and began to chant. *Baby, baby, baby...*

"Fine," she gave in, quietening her inner critic. She knew Maggie would behave because she'd been raised to.

Declan's answering grin should have been a ray of sunshine, but it only made her feel more uneasy. "Thanks, darlin'." He cupped her opposite cheek with his hand and pressed a kiss to the one closest to him.

"But no alcohol, or drugs, or smoking—or parties," she stipulated, dodging Declan's attempt at a second kiss. "Or people over at all, actually. No leaving the house, and--" she warned, looking at Declan seriously, "If anything *does* happen I expect you to discipline him."

Declan nodded. "Fair enough."

They dried their hands and moved into the living room, the noise of Gabe's shoot 'em up video game muted by the huge headphones he had clapped over his ears. When he noticed Rosie standing by the door in his peripheral vision, he did a double-take and then paused the game. He slid his headphones off his head reluctantly.

"Hey," she said, walking further into the room. "You still okay with staying home with Maggie?"

"Sure," he said off-handedly with a half shrug. "No

big deal." But Rosie could see a spark of interest in his eyes, before he turned away from her and focused his attention back on his video game. "It'll be fun."

"Thanks, Gabe. We appreciate it." Rosie said, glancing at Declan, who cleared his throat like he was about to make an important speech.

"Can ya pause your game for a second there, mate?" Declan said. Gabe sighed, took another two sniper shots and then paused the game. He turned on the couch with deliberate slowness to look at both Declan and Rosie.

"Yeah?"

There's a few rules that need to be followed," he said, laying them out. As Declan finished, Maggie trotted into the hall.

"Fine," Gabe said, glancing at Rosie and then shrugging a shoulder. "Can I go back to my game now? I need to get my stats up."

"Okay," Declan nodded.

Rosie turned to Maggie. "We've decided that you can stay here with Gabe," she began, but she was interrupted by a loud whoop that Gabe pointedly ignored.

"But—," Rosie continued, "there are rules, and you have to follow them. And Gabe is in charge. Okay?"

"Okay," Maggie agreed, her grin full of barely contained excitement.

"HELLO, *FUTURE* MRS. BISHOP." ROSIE BEAMED AT Tammy, who had just opened her front door. Dressed in a classy-but-sweet floral maxi dress that really projected Mosswood summer vibes, Tammy looking *amazing*. It was almost enough to make Rosie wish for an engagement herself: she didn't think her skincare routine would ever be *that* good.

"Fancy seein' you here," Tammy teased, standing to the side to make way for her friend.

"Ugh," Rosie grunted, rolling her eyes exaggeratedly as she stepped into the foyer.

"What?" Tammy asked with a light frown, lifting a perfectly manicured hand to pat protectively at her hair.

"You have that 'My skin has a perfect ethereal glow 'cos I'm so in *love*' look," Rosie sighed, as though it were the hardest thing in the world to bear witness to. "*Rude.*"

Tammy smiled at the compliment, but her empathy was evident in the hand she rubbed Rosie's arm with as they marched towards the kitchen. "Things still rough around the edges at home?" she asked, concerned.

"We're not talkin' about that today," Rosie declared, forcing herself to abandon that ship in the middle of its rough seas. "Today is about *you*, and it's a chance for *me* to forget my troubles and focus on my best friend's wedding."

"Okay," Tammy said, clearly grateful. She nodded at Rosie, also just as clearly not backing down on her part of the best-friend bargain. "But we're drinking about *your* troubles next weekend, so set aside an evening."

"Deal," Rosie grinned, entering Tammy's Pinterest-worthy, country-styled kitchen. It was all white-on-white, with a pot of ivy that had been a Christmas gift from Rosie spreading its bright green tendrils up one wall and over the ceiling above the sink. It was thriving, which pleased Rosie. But what got her attention was the kitchen counter, which was full to overflowing with stacks of bridal magazine.

"I might have gone a little overboard," Tammy admitted sheepishly, bustling into the heart of her domain.

"Just a *smidge*," Rosie teased with a grin, settling herself on a stool at the counter. Spoiled for choice, she took up the nearest magazine and began to thumb idly through the pages.

"Coffee?" Tammy asked, getting out two mugs on auto-pilot. Whereas the mugs at Fox Cottage were a rat-tag team of misfits, Tammy's mugs were white porcelain artfully fired in a kiln to look tastefully rustic.

Rosie nodded enthusiastically. "Please!"

"Cake?"

Rosie gasped. "It hurts me that you even need to *ask*." Tammy smirked and set about cutting two thick slices of hummingbird cake.

"So what are we focusing on today?" Rosie asked, glossing over an image of a bride dressed in black—*so* not Tammy—but stopping to look at a pretty pastel pink floral table display.

"I thought we'd decide on the wedding colors, and some styles to look at for the bridesmaid dresses," Tammy said, obviously thrilled to give direction. "And then we could look at some invitations? Only on account of us wantin' to have the wedding sooner rather than later."

"Sounds like a plan," Rosie agreed, shifting magazines to make room for the mugs and cake as Tammy joined her. She gestured at the magazines. "Where'd you get all these?"

"You know Sophie Greenway?" Tammy asked, clearly expecting Rosie to nod.

"Doesn't ring a bell," she replied pleasantly instead.

"Oh!" Tammy placed a hand on her heart, which was a sure-fire sign that she was about to gush over something. "She runs Blush Bridal—a bridalwear boutique—right from her livin' room!" She sighed, lifting her mug. "Sophie's an absolute *queen* with a sewing machine, and she had all these magazines at her house for customers to look at. And," Tammy added, making it clear that she'd saved the best for last, "she offered me a 25% off discount if I order my dresses through her!"

"Wow," Rosie said, looking a little closer at the quality of the magazines. "That's so kind of her!"

"It's *very* kind of her," Tammy agreed, pleased as punch. "She's been a member of the Church for years.

Honestly, I've just been blown away by folks offerin' to help out, either with discounts or things totally for free!" She paused. "I won't hear about not payin' our way. People still have businesses to run and all. But it's so sweet and thoughtful."

Rosie thought it probably didn't hurt that Tammy was marrying the local Pastor, who was the next best thing to God Himself according to most people in town.

"Sounds like the whole town is just thrilled that you and Myles are tying the knot," Rosie smiled. "As they should be."

"Thanks, hon," Tammy said, the apples of her cheeks pinkening. "I'll admit that there has been more support than I thought there would be. I feel so bad for not giving them much credit to begin with. And I'm so grateful! We've had offers from more people than I thought I *knew*. It's been very humbling."

Tammy's exuberance was overshadowed by something else for a moment. A silent moment came to perch on top of the magazine stack on the counter, and Rosie frowned. "... but?"

Tammy's happiness crumpled visibly, her bottom lip lifting and her brows dipping into a frown. "But..." she began, "Matthew has made it perfectly clear that he doesn't approve of the wedding. Or me."

That little jerk.

"What?" Rosie asked indignantly. "Why?"

"I suspect part of it is that he feels I take Myles'

attention away from him," Tammy sighed. "And the other part is loyalty to his mama."

It was reasonable that he'd be feeling both those things, and Rosie hated that she couldn't just claim he was being a brat and make her friend feel better.

"I guess," she admitted begrudgingly, "I know he's still a kid, but he's not a baby. I hope Myles isn't allowing him to get away with bad behavior." Rosie's glance at Tammy invoked a blush from her friend, and her suspicions were confirmed. She desperately wanted to bring up the issues her and Declan had been having with Gabe, and the fact that Gabe and Matthew seemed to have fallen in together. She didn't hold a lot of respect for Matthew Bishop on a good day, but a gnawing worry at the back of her mind began to chew on her conscience. What if Gabe was being a bad influence on Matthew? From what she knew of young Mr. Bishop, he didn't need any help in that department.

"I don't think Myles knows exactly *how* to deal with the situation," Tammy sighed. "According to him, Matthew's been a well-behaved kid until the last year or so. And he always *was* well-behaved—at Church events, anyway. It doesn't help that Prissy has us staked out like a vulture waiting for the relationship to die," she added darkly. "I wouldn't put it past her to be encouraging Matthew to make matters worse."

"I wouldn't put it past her either," Rosie agreed. "*Bitch*."

"Spoiled children are the worst," Tammy sighed, unsettled.

Rosie reached out to squeeze Tammy's hand comfortingly. "They *are*. But I bet he will come around eventually."

Tammy smirked. "I was talkin' about *Prissy*."

Rosie snorted into her mug, pleased that Tammy could keep such a good humor about it and wishing that *she* had that kind of fortitude.

"Enough about her," Rosie said, shuffling to grab a smaller stack of magazines that had bright pink Post-Its flagging some pages. "Show me the dresses you've put markers on!"

Tammy was only too happy to be diverted with a happier topic. "Well," she said with aplomb, flicking through to the first marker. The first dress was a floor-length white chiffon sheath that would have looked almost shapeless, were it not for the beautiful white silk braided belt that gave the whole thing a very Grecian appeal. The model had a fuller figure, just like Tammy, and had paired the dress with simple flat sandals and a pretty pastel floral crown that held the veil.

"*This* one is really romantic? I love the flowy vibe it's got, and it'd be really great for a summer weddin'. I can't think of anything worse than needing to wear a girdle in all that heat!"

"Amen!" Rosie agreed, wanting to break out into a sweat at the very thought of it.

Tammy smiled and flicked to the next one; a more

structured gown that had an empire waistline and a more refined feel to it. It was ivory rather than white, with sleeve caps created with draped strings of pearls and faux diamonds.

"And *this* one is less flowy, but I think I like the lines better," Tammy said, tilting her head to one side as though considering her options. "And it isn't white."

"You're not the one who broke your vows, hon," Rosie reminded her friend, placing a hand on Tammy's. "As far as I'm concerned, you're as pure as the driven snow and you can absolutely wear white if that's what you want to do!"

Tammy's face bloomed with a warm smile. "You're right," she agreed, squeezing Rosie's hand. "Thanks sugar." And then another thought occurred to her. "But I still refuse to wear a girdle."

Rosie grinned. "I'm one hundred percent with you on the 'no girdles' vibe," she promised. She tilted her head in the same direction as Tammy's peering at the last Post-It in that particular magazine with interest. "What's that one?"

"Oh," Tammy said. She was trying to sound nonchalant, but Rosie could detect the note of excitement in her voice. "That one is the one I'm thinking of for the bridesmaids." She smirked cheekily. "Wanna see?"

A little thrill ran up Rosie's spine, tingly and exciting. She had never been a bridesmaid before, let alone a maid of honor. She nudged Tammy playfully with her elbow.

"You tease," she chided as she flipped to the right page. "Oh *Tammy*..."

The gown was a modern take on traditional peach color; deeper and more dusky than a pastel representation of the shade. It transitioned to a dark pink at the hem, truly like the skin of the fruit. It reminded Rosie of sunset on a summer's eve, and she made a mental note to make sure Tammy served peach cocktails at the reception. It was one of those versatile styles with the tie-tops that could be tied in different ways to suit individual body-types, and Rosie absolutely adored it.

"You like it?" Tammy asked nervously, peering at her friend for approval.

"Like it?" Rosie gushed, "I *love* it! That style would be flattering on anyone, and that color is just perfect for a summer wedding! You could have those colors with white in your bouquet - or that flower crown, if you go for that, and tie it all together so well!"

"That just what I was thinking!" Tammy beamed, wriggling on her stool a little with excitement. "I'm glad you approve."

"I'm surprised you thought you needed my approval at all," laughed Rosie. "Everyone in town knows that you're one phone call away from being the style editor at Southern Living!"

"Oh hush," Tammy chuckled, blushing. She ran her fingers over the beautiful bridesmaid dress design.

"I love weddings," Rosie sighed, her hands wrapped around her coffee mug.

"Me too," Tammy confessed with a shy smile. "Though I never thought I would have a *second* one! I'm happy to be wrong."

"I'm pretty happy about that, too," Rosie admitted with a sly grin.

Tammy bumped shoulders with her companionably. "Do you think you'll ever get married again?"

It was a loaded question, and one that Rosie didn't know if she was ready to answer truthfully. She thought about Gabe, and how the sudden addition of a second child changed things. Before, she might have answered that she could see herself getting married again. Now that marrying Declan meant accepting a second child, one who was much more a handful than Maggie, she wasn't so sure. And the more she thought of that, the less she wanted to think about it at all.

"I dunno," she said, feeling the little white lie bury itself just far enough under her skin that it would start to itch before long. "I hadn't really thought about it."

"Well, for the record, I think you and Declan were made for each other," Tammy said, her voice full of emotion. She got up from the counter and went to rinse her mug in the sink, as though doing something practical would stop her from getting overwhelmed. "It's almost like fate, y'know?"

"Yeah," said Rosie softly. "I know exactly what you mean."

With that, Tammy's phone vibrated just once on the counter and made Rosie jump before *Going to the*

Chapel by The Dixie Cups filled the kitchen the same way *Enter Sandman* would fill a stadium at a Metallica concert. Myles' name appeared on the screen.

Tammy dashed forward to scoop it up and take the call. "Hi there, sugar-bear," Tammy began, and Rosie very nearly laughed out loud. "Okay, slow down—you need what now?"

Tammy held one finger up to plug the ear opposite to her phone, as though it might help her hear Myles better. Rosie watched her get paler with each second, until she said a hasty 'Okay,' and ended the call.

"What's wrong?" Rosie asked, already on alert.

"We need to go over to Myles' place," Tammy said, grabbing her house keys so that she could lock the door. "Right now."

It was fortunate that Myles lived just a few doors down from Tammy. The two women dashed down to the sidewalk and then Rosie felt her mouth run dry. The Sheriff's Jeep was parked out front of Myles', lights flashing. Myles was standing on the sidewalk with Sheriff Star, and next to them were Gabe and Maggie. Maggie threaded her fingers together and unthreaded them, eyes on the sidewalk, while Gabe sat on the curb, flicking a lighter with a lid open and closed.

Pending doom bubbled up in Rosie's throat. The pair of them were supposed to at home—Gabe was *supposed* to be watching Maggie! Rosie's pace matched Tammy's as they half-marched, half-ran towards the scene. What the hell had happened *now?*

"What's going on?" Tammy asked, shrill as a cockatoo as she scooted to Myles with concern on her pretty face as she looked him over, and then assessed the children. "Is everyone alright?"

"Yeah, it's fine," Myles told her wryly, "though my siding has definitely seen better days."

The Sheriff rolled her eyes dramatically, muttered some kind of code into the radio attached to her shoulder, and then scribbled on her notepad.

Rosie had come to stand between Gabe and Maggie, who had both taken a step away from her on instinct. Her anger would have been coloring her magical aura right about now, and neither child would be able to deny the trouble they were in. Raw egg dripped down the side of the house—at least two cartons' worth. Rosie's gaze cut angrily to her daughter.

"Egging the Pastor's house?" she asked Maggie in a whisper through gritted teeth. "*Really?*"

"He did it first!" Maggie countered. "Matthew egged *me*. He deserved it!"

Rosie's senses reeled with the incredibly loose logic that children applied to situations.

The Sheriff had been watching this whole exchange with interest. "So, *you're* the one who threw the eggs?" she asked, fixing Maggie with a stare that would have made Judas Iscariot confess just to be out of the line of fire.

But before Maggie could reply, Gabe snorted.

"Like a kid her age could get the eggs that high," he said, crossing his arms.

Maggie's gaze flashed up to Gabriel, her eyebrows knitted into confusion. Gabe's sandy blonde brows lifted, and he shook his head at Maggie just once. She clapped her lips closed. Rosie's mouth fell open.

Sheriff Star looked from Maggie to Gabe and then back again.

"Hrm," the Sheriff murmured thoughtfully, scribbling on her notebook.

At that moment Declan's truck rumbled along The Promenade, pulling up a little roughly at the curb by the Bishop's house.

"What's happenin'?" He said, jumping out of the rusted red Chevrolet. His face was a picture of parental concern, his eyes looking for Gabe in the group. "Are ya okay, lad?" he asked as he approached them all.

Rosie felt her breath stick in her chest as Declan practically ignored Maggie to check on his own kid. Her thoughts must have been reflected on her face, because he glanced at her and then a moment later asked, "Are *you* okay, Mags?"

"Aside from being in trouble with the police, you mean?" Rosie asked, too furious to even give Maggie the chance to speak.

But to her surprise it wasn't Maggie or even Declan

who replied, but Gabe. "She didn't do anything wrong!" he snapped. Rosie spun on him, daring him to say another word. If it wasn't for him, Maggie *wouldn't* have done anything wrong.

"I can't see any need to be writin' them up for such a minor thing," Declan intervened, holding his hands up in a classical 'whoa' response.

"Eggings are often the gateway to more serious offences..." Sheriff Star replied without even a hint of irony. She turned her gaze suspiciously on Gabe. "Like *graffiti* and destruction of property."

"Now, hold on a minute," Myles said, stepping forward. "I'm not the one who called the police, and I'm *not* pressin' charges."

"You didn't?" Rosie's chest flooded with relief to know a man her daughter called Uncle Myles wasn't the one to have called the police on her. Myles, though, flushed until his cheeks were pink even when the blue lights from the police car swung his way.

"No, I didn't." He glanced at Tammy and then at Declan, and then looked at the ground. "It was Matthew."

Gabe snorted, but Rosie felt heat flare up her neck. *Matthew Bishop.* The boy who had egged her and Maggie on the roadside had called the cops when Gabe —and Maggie—came back for some revenge? Typical!

Myles seemed ready to brush it under the rug, though whether it was his own son's discretions or Rosie and Declan's was hard to tell.

"Kids'll be kids," he said, "Lord knows, we can all use a little forgiveness."

His shoulders sank a little as he glanced up at the house towards a window Rosie guessed was Matthew's. The curtains shifted, as though someone had just been peeking through them but retreated for cover.

"*Thank* you Myles," Rosie sighed with relief. Her nerves were in a tangle, and she wasn't sure what else she was feeling except *grateful* that their friend was willing to be reasonable in a bad situation. "I'm so sorry about this—"

"We're sorry about this," Declan added, allowing himself a sideways glance at Gabe.

"Not as sorry as these two are gonna be," Myles replied seriously, slipping his hands into his pockets. "I think it's only fair that we arrange a time for them to come by and clean this up, don't you?"

"Absolutely," Rosie replied, glad to agree to anything that wasn't seeing her kid on bail for a misdemeanor.

But Sheriff Star didn't seem too pleased by the outcome. She had screwed up her face the instant Myles had announced he wasn't going to press charges, and she still looked pinched as she leaned close to speak to him quietly.

"Are you *sure* that's the way you wanna go with this, Pastor?" she asked out of the corner of her mouth, so neither of the concerned parents would think it was meant for them. "Sometimes these kinds of delinquents need a bit of a scare back onto the straight and narrow, if you catch my meaning."

"My daughter is *not* a delinquent," Rosie huffed.

"Neither is my son," Declan added. Declan's dark expression shifted from the Sheriff to Rosie, and he widened his eyes expectantly. Rosie's brows lifted back. He didn't expect her to stick up for *Gabe* in this moment, did he?

The Sheriff hooked a brow at them both. "If you say so." She turned to Myles. "Call me if you change your mind."

"That won't be necessary," Myles told her. The small woman headed for her Jeep. "Thank you so much for your time, Sheriff."

The lights remained on until she was down the street, and Rosie couldn't help but wonder if their new sheriff was going to be as much of a pain in her ass as her predecessor had been. Myles turned to Rosie and Declan.

"Are y'all free tomorrow morning? I'd like to get this off before the sun bakes it on."

Gabe let out a sound that could have been a groan. Rosie's shoulders sank a little at the teen's flagrant complaining.

"Of course," she forced out. "Thanks Myles." She stepped forward and took Tammy's hand. "And sorry that our planning session got ruined."

"Thanks hon," Tammy smiled, though there was sadness in the expression. "I appreciate it." The buoyancy that had been keeping Tammy bobbing on the waves of her upcoming nuptials had flattened into a receding tide. Her friend's shoulders were slumped forward, and Rosie could see bags under Tammy's expertly made-up eyes that she hadn't noticed when they had been gushing over wedding gowns in the kitchen.

"C'mon, you two," Declan said to Maggie and Gabe, nodding his head in the direction of the truck. Rosie really didn't relish the thought of yet another squished family journey home, but she needn't have bothered. Gabe moved back towards the walkway that led to the Bishop's front door.

"I'm going inside to see Matthew," he said matter-of-factly.

"Matthew is grounded," Myles responded. He crossed his arms over his stomach and leaned back, rocking back on his heels and nodding his chin firmly.

Rosie met Tammy's gaze, and Tammy looked to the sky as though asking for patience.

"And so're you," Declan added for good measure, looking at Gabe expectantly before turning his body sideways along the walkway to give the teen space to walk by. Gabe sighed and moved back toward the truck, hands shoved deep into his pockets and his shoulders hunched over deeply.

Rosie hesitated as she watched the two of them head toward the truck, and then she made a split-second decision.

"I'm going to walk home with Maggie."

Maggie looked up at Rosie in alarm and then over at Declan. Her wide eyes pleaded for him not to leave her alone with her mother, but Declan responded to the unspoken plea with a hard face and a nod to Rosie. He got into the truck and closed the door, leaving Rosie alone with a sheepish and quiet Magnolia.

Maggie glanced up at her mother and then back down at her own toes. Rosie pursed her lips into a straight line.

"Let's go, missy."

CHAPTER SIX

The next morning, Maggie stared up at the mess of dried raw egg splattered all over the front of the Bishop's house. Her little nose was wrinkled and her bottom lip was threatening to poke out in a pout.

Rosie had to hand it to Myles. Waiting until the next day had left the eggs sticky and stinky, and it made the job of cleaning up much more unpleasant than it would have been just hosing it off the night before.

Maggie turned to look up at her mother. "Where's Gabe?" she asked.

"I'm not sure." Rosie tapped her phone to check the time.

"I'm not starting until he gets here." Maggie declared, sitting on the porch step in a huff. "It's his punishment too."

"Is it?" Rosie asked lightly. "I thought Gabe didn't throw any of the eggs?"

Maggie glanced sheepishly at her mom. "You caught that, huh?"

Rosie pressed her lips together. "Mmhmm."

"Well I was thinking about it last night after I went to bed," Maggie sighed.

"I know I deserve to be punished, and I *will* clean the house like Uncle Myles said. But I wouldn't have ever decided to do this if *Gabe* hadn't told me that it's important to pay back people who do bad things to you." Maggie frowned, scuffing the toe of her sneaker on the concrete driveway. "I wouldn't have walked down here by myself—*Gabe* came with me. And *he* bought the eggs from the Go-Go."

Rosie's brows lifted, and then fell almost immediately in a frown that matched her daughter's. "Maggie, you're going into middle school at the end of the summer. You're gonna have a lot of people trying to tell you what to do—what will make you *cool*."

Maggie flushed, looking away to the garden bed in a move that told Rosie she'd hit the nail on the head. Wanting your new older stepbrother to think you're cool was only natural at Maggie's age, but doing bad things to achieve that wouldn't fly.

"You're responsible for your own choices," Rosie told her sagely. "And when *you* make a bad choice, *you* have to make it right."

"But Gabe should still be here!" Maggie fired back. "It's not fair!"

Rosie straightened, ready to illustrate her point. "Was it fair of you to throw eggs at *Myles'* house because someone was mean to you a year ago?"

Maggie hesitated, but then realized she didn't have anywhere else to turn with that line of argument. "No."

"Then it is fair that you have more work to do today than you would have otherwise, because you were going to make Myles have to clean this up if you didn't get caught," Rosie pointed out.

She took Maggie's silence as her answer.

"Okay," she said, barely able to hold off on sighing. "Off to the garage to find a bucket, some detergent, and a broom. No more complaining."

"Yes ma'am," Maggie sighed, heading for the garage.

DECLAN AND GABE ARRIVED ABOUT AN HOUR LATER. Maggie downed her soapy broom as Gabe wandered over to her sullenly, and Rosie heard her ask where he'd been. Declan stepped up onto the porch dejectedly.

"He was down by the river with Matthew and their mates," the tall Irishman said, irritation plain on his face as he side-eyed his teenage soon. "Matthew's still there," he said to Myles as an aside, "if you were wonderin' where he got off to."

Myles sighed. "Excuse me," he said as he stood up and pulled his cell phone from his pocket.

"Why don't we head inside?" Tammy suggested. "I'll make some sandwiches for lunch."

"Egg salad?" Rosie asked hopefully, loud enough for Gabe and Maggie to hear.

"You know it!" Tammy winked and followed Myles into the house. Before Declan could follow them, Rosie reached out and put her hand on his bicep to stop him in his tracks. Maggie and Gabe were far enough away that Rosie knew she wouldn't be overheard. She leaned towards him.

"I really don't think it's a great idea for Gabe to keep hanging out with Matthew," she said, her tone colored with concern. "I worry that maybe they bring out the worst in each other. Tammy told me herself that they've been having all kinds of issues with him."

Declan bristled defensively. "What am I supposed to do?" he asked, sounding genuinely despondent beneath his instinct to take his kid's side. "Tell him that he can't be hangin' out with the *Pastor's son?*" He fixed Rosie with a helpless look, and then made to step into the house.

Rosie stopped him again. "You could actually work on spending some time with him, instead of leaving him to his own devices," she suggested, an eyebrow hitched. "Playing video games doesn't equate to bonding, you know."

Declan sighed as the pair of them stepped into the

house. "You're right," he agreed, nodding as the advice sank in. "I'll work something out."

A while later, when tensions had simmered a little and Tammy's famous egg salad sandwiches were sitting pretty on a platter and Myles' perfectly roasted and brewed coffee was a pleasant memory, the talk turned inevitably to Mosswood's upcoming wedding.

"I've called in my friend—one of the leaders from my summer seminary group — to do the ceremony," Myles was saying, gazing at Tammy with a happy twinkle in his bright blue eyes. "Not like I could officiate over my own weddin', is it?" He laughed at his own joke, while Tammy chuckled and Rosie smiled indulgently.

The sound of the side door opening and closing and two pairs of shoes pattering towards the kitchen was enough to make them all turn and look at Maggie and Gabe, who entered the room looking rather pleased with themselves.

"We're done," Gabe smirked, earning him an admiring look from Maggie—who then also smirked.

Rosie quirked a brow. "Are you sure?"

"We're sure," Maggie said, slipping her hands into her pockets in an action that mimicked one of Rosie's habits. "All the egg's gone, and we weeded the garden beds too."

The grownups followed them out to see whether the work passed muster. The outside of the house was spotless once again, with freshly cleaned siding and garden beds that were weed-free. The weeds were piled into the wheelbarrow nearby almost in rows—as though they had been plucked out of the ground by some form of machinery. On closer inspection, it wasn't just the siding that had been egged that was clean. The whole house sparkled from top to bottom... like magic.

"Well, I can't fault that you've got the house looking clean," Myles sighed, looking disappointed. "But how are your consciences doing? Clear?" he asked, levelling a pointed gaze at the two kids, "or a little grimy?"

"What?" Gabe's eyes widened in alarm. One of his blond eyebrows crooked higher as he inspected Myles, looking more than a little suspicious himself.

"Oh, *honey*," Tammy said with a small shake of her head. Somehow, the sympathy in her tone only managed to make the words sound even more devastating.

"They know," Rosie added. She had crossed her arms over her chest, and now she lifted a brow at Gabe and then at Maggie, who avoided her gaze. Gabe sighed heavily, sinking a little in his posture.

Declan shook his head, too, though perhaps for different reasons than Tammy. "Ya didn't even try, mate. We can feel ya magic everywhere."

It was true. Traces of their magical influence were all over the house and yard, like invisible snail trails. But Rosie wondered if Declan was disappointed in the act itself or just the execution of it.

"When Matthew came out to Fox Cottage to work off his punishment, he had to work hard all day," Myles reminded them. "Y'all finished in less than half an hour because you cheated."

"I can't believe you would do this," Rosie agreed. She took a deep breath, letting it fill her lungs entirely, before releasing it and then turning to Myles.

"I'm so sorry, Myles. How about if we bring them over next weekend? You'll have more weeds to pull by then, and the lawns'll need mowing. And I will personally sit on a chair on the driveway to supervise them."

Gabe and Maggie threw horrified glances at each other, but Myles just shrugged and shook his head in a way that was decidedly un-Myles-like.

"I dunno," he sighed. "If we can't trust them to do the punishment that's been given to them, I'm not sure there's a point." His phone beeped in his pocket, and he reached for it. When he saw whatever was on the screen, his shoulders tensed, and his expression became harder. "We'll have to talk about this later."

Rosie glanced at Tammy, who widened her eyes as though to say, *See?*

"You two," Declan said, jerking his head in the direction of the truck as Myles left to go get his son. "Get in."

"I'll see you on Monday," Tammy said.

"Bye," Rosie said solemnly to her friend, mustering up a ghost of a smile for Tammy's benefit.

"Don't let yourself get worked up, love," Declan said as soon as they were alone. He glanced at the kids heading for the truck and offered Rosie his signature crooked half-smile. "They're witches! What else were you expecting?"

It was the final straw for her. She glared up at Declan.

"I'm expecting my decisions and opinions to be respected, by everyone who lives under my roof, no *matter* their age." She locked her gaze onto his pointedly.

His face fell. "I probably deserve that," he said, his tone soft and apologetic.

"Yeah, you do!" she agreed. But he was being apologetic, so she took a deep breath to soothe her nerves.

"Take the kids home," she told him, her tone reconciliatory. "I'll meet you there later."

"You sure?" he asked, as though it might be a trap she was setting to snap him with later.

She nodded. "There are only three seatbelts," she pointed out.

Declan pressed his lips together. His expression was disappointed and down, like the number of seatbelts in the truck somehow equated to the number of spaces left in their lives for family members. He lowered his gaze a moment later, and then he nodded.

With the rest of the Fox Cottage household taken care of, Rosie turned her attention to the long walk home on black asphalt in the heat. She let her shoulders sag forward and her head roll back in a body language expression not unlike that of the two kids who had just left.

Ugh.

Rosie took the long way home, walking all the way down Lee Street, through the park and past the stately fountain of General Beaufort Moss. Mosswood's founder, gazed determinedly at the river he had decided to build a town around, while pigeons gathered around him like a loyal band of soldiers. Rosie would have enjoyed the serenity of the afternoon if it hadn't been too hot of a day and *she* hadn't been too hot under the collar. By the time she'd walked along the entire waterfront she was still too angry to go home.

But she didn't have anywhere else to be, and her responsibilities were weighing heavily on her mind. She set out along the highway, waving flies away from her face and squinting into the hazy distance. Sweat trickled down the back of her neck, and she wished that she'd thought to put her hair into a ponytail that morning instead of letting it hang around her face.

Pausing by the dry ditch in front of the old mill, Rosie bent to pluck a long reed left over from Spring. It was brown and sinewy, and it didn't take her much magic at all to tie it into a circle and elasticate it enough to serve as a temporary hair tie. She stood in the shade of the building gratefully, the breeze working its own magic to cool her down a degree or two in both temperature and temperament.

She glanced up at the old brick pile, imagining what the mill must have been like in its hey-day. It would have supported more than half the town, no doubt, and it was a shame that whoever did own the building had let it fall into such disrepair. And to add insult to injury, there was a giant dick still painted atop the brick—a huge metaphorical bird flipped at the town and the hard-working folk who had built it.

Rosie couldn't stand to look at it any longer. She drew in her magic, pulling from the area that was still ripe with the energy of Gabe's residual magic. She channeled it all towards having a little love for the building that had been her milestone during her long walks to town and back; to the building that had once been a pillar of the community she had chosen to call home. As she let go of her magic, her irritation wouldn't be soothed by a gradual and steady release.

It came in a short, sharp burst instead, and the paint scrambled away from the walls like vermin being eradicated. It popped into the air in a shower of pink flakes, before vanishing from existence. She continued to focus her energy on different parts of the 'artwork', until all trace of it was gone and there was just a stalwart brick wall left there in its stead. The old Hayes Sugar and Syrup logo was still barely visible, and for a moment Rosie was tempted to restore it to its former glory—before reminding herself how suspicious that would be. She'd already taken matters into her own hands by removing the graffiti. It was time to leave well enough alone and return to her own little patch of burweed growing back at Fox Cottage.

As she wandered up The Ridge and through the start of the woods towards home, Rosie took her sweet time, partly because she was tired from releasing her pent-up anger, partly because she had used magic. As she wandered out onto the gravel driveway that led up to the cottage, she noticed a small figure in the distance, slumped into the tire swing that Declan had hung from the huge oak tree in the middle of the lawn. Rosie moseyed on over, taking her time, and came to halt just a few yards away.

"Hey," she said. The walk and the magical release had leeched most of the anger out of her, and now she just felt a mother's deep-seated need to heal everything.

"Hey," Maggie said back, her voice small. She didn't look up to meet her mother's gaze, and she fidgeted with the rope she was hanging on to. Letting the swing wind down, Maggie waited until it was almost at a standstill before asking "Why don't you like Gabe?"

Yikes. Rosie wasn't sure how to even approach this subject but seeing that Maggie was astute enough to ask it in the first place, she figured the least she could do was be honest. She sat on the lawn by the swing, considered it for a moment, and then met her daughter's inquiring gaze.

"It's not that I don't like *him* personally," she sighed with a shrug. "I just don't like the way he's behaving." She paused, debating whether to continue, but then she took a deep breath and admitted something a little deeper than she had yet. "And I don't like seeing his influence on *you*."

Maggie frowned lightly. "What do you mean?"

Rosie paused, trying to think of how to word this. But she decided just to be honest.

"Someday, Maggie, sooner than either of us know, you will start to question whether the decisions I make for you are the same ones you would make for yourself. And when that happens, you will have to decide how to face that, whether you will decide to lie to me and sneak around, or fight and be angry, or whether you will come to me and talk about it and try to work it out with me."

She looked up at her daughter. Though she could still look five or six, when she put her covers over her head and pretended to be a wizard in the forests, she could also look very grown up. Right now, with the sunset highlighting the way her baby fat was disappearing from her cheeks and the light in her hair making a halo around her face, she could almost be called a young woman.

"The other day you followed Gabe and snuck around throwing eggs at Myles' house. And when you were caught, you got angry." Without the anger of the situation to bolster her, Rosie felt a stinging at the corner of her eyes. "I hope you know you can always talk to me when you disagree with me, and you don't have to sneak around or lie. I hope you'll always try."

Maggie looked down, and with just that small shift,

she looked small and young again, cheeks full and round, and eyelashes long against her cheeks.

"Yeah," she agreed with her mother. "I should have talked to you. I'm sorry."

Rosie swallowed down the lump in her throat, feeling relief flow through her veins for what seemed like the first time since Gabe had arrived. Her little girl was still her little girl, at least for one more moment.

Maggie was quiet for a long pause, as though letting the conversation sink in fully. And then she glanced up. "What will happen if Gabe keeps behaving the way he's behaving?"

Rosie would have loved to know the answer herself, because none of the ones she had been passing around in her mind—not the least of which was losing Declan —were very pleasant to think about. She chewed the inside of her lip for a moment, then looked back at her daughter again.

"Honestly?" She shrugged. "I don't know, Pumpkin. I wish I did. But these things are hard to work out, sometimes."

Maggie still peered at her, in that way she sometimes had which made her look wise beyond her years. She spoke again.

"Will you make him leave?"

Rosie froze. She froze in her limbs and she froze in her heart. Her lips parted long before she had any words to pass between them.

"I don't know," she finally admitted.

Maggie's hands curled around the rope of the tire swing. "Will Declan leave?"

Rosie had to push back the burning sensation in her eyes again and shook her head. "I don't know that either, Pumpkin."

Maggie looked at the ground and pushed off with her toes, making the tire swing slightly on the rope. Rosie took in a shaky breath, then stood, dusting off the back of her jeans.

"But you know what I do know?" she said as she rose.

Maggie took her mom's signal and began to disentangle herself from the swing. "What?"

"I know no matter what happens, they're going to be okay, and so are we. Okay?"

For a moment or two, the only sound was the crickets singing. And then Maggie nodded, sidling up to Rosie and placing an arm around her mother's waist. "Okay Mom."

"Okay." Rosie slipped her arm around Maggie's shoulders, leading them towards the porch. "Now let's go inside, before the mosquitos carry us off."

CHAPTER SEVEN

L ow, melodic tunes wafted through the air. Nourish was Rosie's sanctuary.

Well. Some things were still a work in progress.

Rosie cleared the tables in the dining room that had been abandoned by the 6am coffee crowd, making way for anyone looking for a hearty mid-week breakfast. The cafe was usually busiest in the mornings, and that suited Rosie right down to the ground. She finished stacking dishes onto her tray and wiped the table as the conversation from a table by the windows drifted over to her.

"Not just the mailboxes," Earl, the portly man with a full lumberjack beard who ran the Mosswood Post Office was saying. "Milly down at the Sheriff's Department told me that they found empty beer bottles all over the dock down by the river—some of 'em smashed up."

Rosie froze, her blood running cold. Gabe hadn't

come home the other night, which until now had been making Rosie worry for his safety. But if he had been out causing havoc all over town, knocking down mailboxes and who knows what else, she could not vouch for her temper. Desperate to hear more, she momentarily left the dishes and opted to take up a nearby watering can instead. She began to water the peace lilies she had in a square terracotta pot nearby, homing in on the conversation.

"Disgraceful," tutted Beverly Brown. "It's gettin' warm enough to swim, and all the kids gather 'round that dock. Someone's gonna get cut to ribbons!"

Grace Simmons, who had been the principal at the Elementary School way back when and still lived in a cottage down by the rocky rapids on the river, leaned closer to the group. "Well I heard people partying out on the falls until all hours of the mornin'," she said, pursing her whole face up like she was drinking straight lemon juice and not one of Tammy's perfect vanilla lattes.

"So did I!" Earl agreed in an overly-excited whisper. "Kept me and Alice awake until almost dawn!" He frowned. "Damned inconsiderate, if you ask me!"

Rosie moved on to watering the ivy by the door, determined to get closer.

Grace sighed, folding her frail arms and sitting back in her chair. "I'll tell ya, I dunno what this town is comin' to, these days." She shook her head. "Children runnin' wild all hours of the night, unsupervised. I never would have permitted such tomfoolery when I was in charge!"

Beverly patted her hand sympathetically, and Earl dipped his head sagely. "It's because of all the blow-ins we've had recently," he declared in a low voice, "if you take my meanin'."

At that, all three of them turned to glance in Rosie's direction before turning their attention back to the table.

"Oh, I know exactly what you mean, Earl," Beverly sniffed, not bothering to try and keep her voice low to spare Rosie's feelings. "I was walkin' Pepper up along The Crescent the other day, and I saw raw egg *all over* Pastor Bishop's house!"

"No!" Earl gasped, as though this news was right up there with the headlines that JFK had been assassinated.

"Yes, sir, I did," Beverly reiterated with a drawn-out nod. "And let's not *any* of us forget about the giant *vulgar* monstrosity at the Mill—"

Rosie had heard enough. She plonked the watering can down a little louder than she had meant to, collected the dishes from the table she had abandoned and made a beeline for the kitchen. It seemed everyone was talking about her and her family in a way they hadn't in a long while—and all because of Gabe.

Tammy glanced up from decorating a batch of sugar cookies in the shapes of summer flowers as Rosie burst through the kitchen door.

"Those are works of art," she breathed, bending to take a closer look at a delicately contrived Angelonia.

"They're just sugar cookies," Tammy said dismissively with a blush.

"There is nothing 'just sugar cookies' about them" Rosie insisted. "Whatever price you were thinking about putting on them—double it."

Tammy smiled appreciatively, kneading the small of her back with her knuckles. "Deal. Everythin' okay, hon? You've got a face like a thundercloud."

"The Town Council is in fine form this morning," Rosie complained under her breath to her friend, sliding the dishes onto the draining board by the sink. "It's a wonder they even wanted to come in here at *all*, the way they're riled."

Tammy pressed her lips together in a sympathetic smile and went back to concentrating on her cookies. "Well, there's no way of tellin' who's behind it all," she said, but a note in her voice told Rosie that she had her own personal views on the matter and was just too kind to voice them. "But I have to say it is unsettlin'. I don't know how I even feel about planning a weddin' with all the troubles happening around town."

She sighed, finishing one cookie with a flourish of her piping bag. "Maybe we really oughtta postpone it until next year after all. I don't know what I was thinking—*this* summer really is very soon."

Rosie's indignation at overhearing gossip about her and her family was kicked in the guts by Tammy's admission, and it was her first instinct to buck. Tammy was such a warm and wonderful person—more sister than friend—and Rosie would be damned if she was going to let Gabriel ruin a wedding that meant so much to her nearest and dearest.

"Don't you even think of it," Rosie told her.

Tammy turned to lean against the counter with a sheepish expression. "But what will they think about Myles as a town leader if he can't even keep his own son in line?"

She hated to admit it, but she hadn't thought of that, or of anything other than the trouble Gabriel acting out was making for *her*. But Tammy was right. How *did* it look for the entire town to be gossiping not just about Declan's kid, but about the *Pastor's?* Especially when that pastor was putting together a wedding.

If her face had looked like a thundercloud before, she could only imagine it now looked like a hurricane. It just wasn't *fair*. Why was everyone in this town paying for Gabriel's mistakes but Gabriel?

Suddenly, something inside of her steeled over and she reached behind her for the tie on her apron.

"I hate to ask, but would you mind if I leave early?" she asked hopefully. She felt bad leaving Tammy to it, but needs must.

"Of course, I don't," Tammy said, plucking up four cookies from her stockpile and laying them out carefully on a plate. "Take these with you—for the family," she said before adding a wise nod. "A little sweetness never hurt a sour situation."

F OX C OTTAGE WAS QUIET AS A MOUSE WHEN R OSIE LET herself in. It was almost lunch. Maggie was at a friend's house, and Declan was at work with Gabe. Rosie didn't have an afternoon shift at the Go-Go Mart, which meant she could to do what needed to be done.

She didn't waste any time. She locked the front door, dumped her purse on the wall hook by the door and put the plate of cookies on the side table beneath it before stepping straight into the living room. In typical teenage boy style, Gabe's belongings were strewn everywhere. It was yet another matter of contention between her and Declan—if Maggie was expected to keep her space tidy, then Gabe should be as well. Rosie frowned as she stepped over an inside-out pair of jeans on the floor, the expression deepening at the line of used glasses that had been stashed on the mantlepiece below the huge TV Declan had bought.

Totally unacceptable. But not what she was looking for.

She began lifting the couch cushions one at a time, peering into the void under them as though she might find Jimmy Hoffa hiding under there. Nothing. Pushing them back into place, she looked under the couch and was assaulted by the stench of week-old socks. She backed out quickly, took a breath, and then decided to open the drapes and the window.

And there, tucked behind the drapes by the ancient

lamp that sat in the corner, was a ratty old backpack that Rosie hadn't noticed until then. Suspicion pooled in her guts, and she suddenly knew that she'd hit the jackpot. Kneeling on the carpet, Rosie carefully opened the backpack and peered inside.

Stale beer and cigarette smoke exploded like a bomb in her face. Her fingers closed around an aerosol can that she lifted to inspect. Bubblegum pink paint drips stained the spray nozzle and the can itself, which felt almost empty. Her anger grew when she also found a bottle of lighter fluid, undoubtedly for the stupid lighter that he kept flicking in everyone's faces.

Rosie dug deeper into the bag. Her fingers had just closed around something that felt awfully like a metal mailbox number when she heard keys being jingled in the lock of the front door, followed by two male voices conversing pleasantly. Declan was the only person who had keys to the house apart from her. Rosie's mouth fell open in shock and dismay—which soon turned to horror as she realized she was about to be caught red-handed trying to catch *Gabe* red-handed.

Rosie panicked. She shoved the can of spray-paint and bottle of lighter fluid back into the bag without care for how she had taken them out and zipped up the whole thing with a 'zwoop!' that was way louder than she had hoped it would be. She was just scrambling to her feet when Declan and Gabe came through the front door.

"Trust me," Declan laughed. He sounded *happy*— which is something that he hadn't sounded for a while.

"I *know* him. And he's a bit of a prat, but a totally decent boxer."

"No way. Mad-Dog Morrigan'd thrash Kanga Copeland any day," Gabe countered with a disbelieving chuckle, which fell silent as he and his dad rounded the corner into the living room. Declan started when he noticed Rosie was already in the house.

"Hey, love," he said, pleasantly surprised—for now. "What're ya doin' home? I thought you were gonna be with Tammy at Nourish until this afternoon!"

Gabe's gaze landed on Rosie, and then fell to look at his exposed backpack. His green eyes narrowed and his expression darkened. "She was going through my stuff."

Declan looked at Gabe as though he might be joking, and then his attention turned to Rosie when he realized that it wasn't a joke at all. "Rosie?" he asked. "Is he right?"

Fuck. She had nowhere to go with this except to tell the truth, and she knew it. But before she had a chance to answer Declan, Gabriel threw up his hands angrily.

"Of course, I'm right!" He glared at Rosie, his jaw clenching and unclenching and his nostrils flared. "She's wanted me out of here since the moment I fucking arrived!"

"Hey," Declan intervened, holding a hand up as though to steady his kid's temper. "Lower your voice and leave out the swearin'. No matter *what*, you don't speak to her like that—you got me?"

But Gabe had stopped listening. He transferred his

weight from one foot to the other restlessly, looking like a caged animal desperate to escape.

"Should've *known* you'd take her side," he spat, "You're just like mum! All you care about is that stupid prophecy."

"Gabe—" Declan started, but he was too late. Gabe lunged forward, scooping up his evidence-filled back-pack before storming out of the front door. He slammed it behind him, rattling the glass in its panes.

Declan stared at the door for a long moment, as though he didn't want to turn back around and face Rosie. But eventually, he couldn't avoid looking at her any longer. He swiveled back, his mossy green eyes hurt and accusing when she met them.

"I'm sorry," she said softly. "I know I shouldn't have—"

"No," Declan barked, cutting her off. "You shouldn't have. But ya *did*." He had never used such a harsh tone with her before, and while she wasn't scared of earning his displeasure when she thought she was right, being censured now was far worse, because she was no longer sure she was.

He shook his head with disappointment. "He *already* feels unwelcome. And ya had t'go an' make that worse by riflin' through his belongings?" he pressed his lips together before he released a long breath. "What exactly did y'think you were gonna find, Rosie?"

Her shame boiled dry. "Only things that I *did* find!"

she fired back, "like the spray-paint he used at the Mill!"

Declan scoffed, rolling his eyes. "You're *completely* overreactin'," he said. "Boys are different to girls—I can tell ya right now that I raised more hell five times over when I was a lad than anythin' Gabe might—or might *not*—have done since gettin' here. And Maggie isn't even a teenager yet! You'll see."

"Sorry," Rosie snapped back sarcastically. "I didn't realize that three solid weeks of half-assed parenting qualified you to tell other parents how it's done."

Declan stiffened. He sniffed and then took a deep breath.

"That's unfair," he told Rosie quietly, "and you know it."

He was right. But in that way that arguments sometimes devolved into one mean thing being hurled after another, she had fallen into the trap of letting her frustrations fly out of her mouth.

"It is unfair," she agreed. "Just like you saying that I am overreacting is unfair. This house has been in turmoil since he got here, and now the town is heading that way too! Gabe needs a firmer hand than you're giving him, and I'm worried about what'll happen if he doesn't get it."

"Even if he does," Declan said stoically, grabbing his keys, "you said we'd decide those things together. You said you'd help. This—" He pointed to the place where Gabe's bag had once sat, keys jingling as he gestured. "—isn't helping."

He turned through the doorway and his heavy footsteps pounded down the few short steps to the ground. Rosie turned in a circle in the middle of the small living room, her mind turning circles, too. She plopped onto the sagging couch and let her forehead fall into her hands.

Now what?

CHAPTER EIGHT

The sound of Declan's truck rumbling up the driveway towards Fox Cottage had come to be a sound Rosie associated with happiness. Though they had been seeing each other for a while now a little thrill would still tickle the inside of her stomach, and she'd usually find herself drifting to the door so that she could greet him when he came in. But tonight the sound smothered the already-heavy feeling of anxiety she felt in her very core. She didn't know what emotions were going to walk through that door with her boyfriend and his son, and the thought worried her.

Maggie was doing her homework at the kitchen counter and hadn't even looked up, oblivious to the inner turmoil currently holding her mother hostage. Rosie looked at her for a second, wondering if she should send Maggie to her room so that she would be out of the line of fire. And then her gaze fell to the plate of perfect cookies Tammy had sent her home with.

A little sweetness never hurt a sour situation. Maggie was the sweetest thing in the house, so maybe she'd better keep her around.

She had put four plastic tumblers on the counter earlier while prepping dinner, and now she poured a little milk—just enough for dipping and washing down a cookie—in each. Declan and Gabe came through the door. Rosie took a deep breath and hoped that Tammy's culinary skills were enough to garnish the olive branch she had dished up. Gabe came into the kitchen first. He glanced at the cookies and milk before flicking his blonde mane out of his eyes.

Rosie could hear Declan hovering in the hallway just outside of the kitchen doorway, which made her heart ache. She hated the situation they were in right now, and though she wanted to just be able to use her magic and fix it all, she knew she couldn't. Relationships were tough. Parenting was tough. Putting them both together and adding a teenager who had enough angst to fill an oil tanker was a recipe for a perfect storm.

When he decided to enter the room Declan's face was serious, like a piece of marble used for practice by a master sculptor. His slightly crooked and too-big nose looked as though it was a support for his currently heavy brow, which was creased into a frown. His lips, that Rosie was so used to seeing curved up in his sexy, roguish grin, were flat and humorless. But when he saw the cups and cookies on the counter, his expression softened and some tension melted out of his broad shoulders.

"What's all this then?" he asked Rosie lightly, but she could tell from his reaction that he knew her next move already.

She shrugged a shoulder, as though it would be enough to prompt her into a further explanation. "I just thought we could all use a moment together as a family," she said simply, her eyes meeting his. An unspoken word passed between them, carried forward as their individual magical auras reached out to each other tentatively.

Sorry.

Gabriel was watching them intently from his vantage point at the table. The color of his eyes was so much like Declan that Rosie often found herself startled by it. He sat back in his chair, the ripped knees of his jeans jutting out from beneath the table as he lounged. He said nothing, but his gaze was as intent as a National Geographic writer as he watched Declan give Rosie a quick but promising kiss.

"Thanks, darlin'," he said softly, a hint of his smile teasing the corner of his lips. "It's a lovely thought. Did you make these?" he asked, impressed, as he bent to inspect the cookies.

"Aunt Tammy did," Maggie interjected with an excited wiggle on her stool, like a puppy who had been waiting for a treat. "Can I have my cookie *now*, Mom?"

Rosie nodded, and the cookies were demolished in record time. Even Gabe came over to have his, though he didn't speak. Rosie and Declan made polite chatter, and Maggie was none the wiser to the low grumble of thunder hovering just below the surface of this otherwise happy scene. Before long, though, it couldn't be stretched out any longer.

"Thank you both for a lovely snack," Declan said to Rosie with a smile, before looking back at Gabe. "Us lads'll do the washing up, won't we Gabe?"

Obviously unimpressed with his father's offer, Gabe shrugged. He hadn't spoken since they had come back home but had watched them all with a closeness that set Rosie's nerves on edge. She felt as though he was taking inventory, but she didn't know what for.

"I think I'll start getting ready for bed while you guys finish up," she said as she stood. She placed a hand on Maggie's shoulder as she squeezed past the back of her chair. "Why don't you go get ready for bed too, Mags, and then I'll come tuck you in."

"You still get tucked in?" Gabe asked Maggie as he reached to finish his glass of milk.

"…Yeah," Maggie replied. Rosie felt her heartbeat grow heavier at the way Maggie toed the floor in embarrassment, and had to forcibly take a deeper breath when Declan cleared his throat at the sink.

"Can't I stay up just a little longer?" Maggie asked hopefully. *"Please?"*

"No, ma'am," Rosie said gently.

Rosie was halfway to her bedroom when she heard a loud knock at the door. "I'll get it!" she called back over her shoulder, heading to unlock and open the front door only to find that there was no one there. And then she saw it.

The taunting flicker of flames caught her eye, and Rosie gasped. There, scorching the cute custom 'Fox Cottage' doormat Tammy had made for her, was a burning brown paper bag. Her mouth fell open and then snapped closed again at the smell—or more accurately, *taste*—of the bag's contents. She leaned out of the door as far as she could to try and see whoever it was who'd left it, but the darkness had swallowed them up. Acutely aware that whoever it was would be hiding to watch the outcome of their prank, Rosie scowled until Declan appeared behind her.

"Fuckin' hell!" he exclaimed, reaching for the broom next to the front door on instinct.

"No—" Rosie began, but she was too late, and she knew it.

Declan swung with his considerable might, squashing the bag which popped with gusto. There was an explosion, and Rosie stiffened as she felt something warm and slimy splatter all over her ankle.

It was on her clothes. It was all over the porch. It was the most disgustingly pungent dog poop she had ever smelled in her entire life, and it was covering her, her door, and anywhere in and outside the house where it had a clear angle. It even dropped a bit from the porch overhang. Pieces of burning bag and flaming biohazard fell from the air and onto the porch floor, somehow smelling even *worse* than just the dog poop on its own.

"*Ugh!!*"

Declan brushed past her as he fled out of the door, leaping over the porch railing to desperately swipe dog crap onto the grass beyond. As she stood nose-deep in abject horror and just watched, two sets of running footsteps sounded behind her. Dueling groans of disgust and cackles of laughter began to crop up like the first few pops of popcorn in a boiler.

"Well," Gabe said as he tiptoed past Rosie onto the porch to get a look at the damage. He carefully avoided every pile and drip as he spun to check it out. "That's *shitty.*"

Rosie's ribcage ceased moving, torn between correcting the cursing and admiring the pun. Maggie didn't have such compunctions and squealed with laughter. Rosie did *not* see the humor, but at the way Maggie and Gabe cackled, a snort escaped her anyway. And she *instantly* regretted it. Breathing through her nose was *not a thing* in this situation. *Not a thing at all.*

"Alright, move, Gabe," Declan called from somewhere in the darkness. Dutifully, Gabe stepped off the porch and into the grass beyond. But while he had been clever enough to duck for cover, Rosie was *not*. The first burst of water from Declan and his water hose shot across the porch, full of built-up pressure from the day's heat and the open spiggot. It watered down whatever was on the porch and then splashed back up onto Rosie's exposed leg, taking the poop quotient from calf to floor, up to the top of her knees. She jumped and squealed.

"*DECLAN!*"

"Whoops!" Declan said in the darkness, the sound of an accidental smile in his voice.

Gabriel's laughter turned into a flat giggle that elongated the syllable that escaped him, "Ewwwwww!"

Rosie did not, in any way shape or form, at all approve of *poop related shenanigans*. But with poop water dripping down her bare legs and two half-grown humans cackling at her predicament, she wasn't feeling particularly generous. So she grabbed Declan's disastrous weapon-of-choice and *swept* some of the leftover debris his way through the banister around the porch.

"Augh!" He spun in place, raising his arms to cover his important points. "That's disgusting!!"

"*I know!*" By this point, even Rosie had half a smile blending into her horrified expression. Revenge was as sweet as it was stinky.

Gabriel had completely lost control of himself on the lawn. His laugh had gone from controlled and cool teen, to intensifying giggle, and now it had reached its peak: a high-pitched guffaw that fluctuated in both power and octaves. The sound was so addictive, Declan quickly followed suit.

"You think that's funny?" he called. A moment later, a well-aimed shot of water blasted his son in the stomach.

"No!! Not the shirt!" Gabe was up like a shot and took the steps to the porch in one leap, but Rosie threw her arms out across the door to stop him coming in.

"Oh no you don't!"

"Gah!" Gabe turned to vault back over the side of the porch and avoid his father that way, and Rosie called after him into the night.

"No one comes into this house until you are rinsed of *all* filth!"

She should have thought her words through. Declan's voice carried back to her. "Oh yeah?"

"*No.*"

It was too late. It was far too late. Rosie darted down the porch steps and onto the lawn to avoid Declan's water stream, her voice stuttering with every running step.

"Sto-o-o-o-op!"

Declan had the upper hand until Maggie snuck out and kinked the hose to stop his reign of terror. By the time they had each had their turn as king of the garden hose, Rosie was no longer concerned about the poop on them, because they were all so soaked through that nothing could have survived.

"Alright now," Declan called at last. "No more play-ing! Let me get this porch cleaned up."

The three of them waited for him to do the poop

squirting. As they waited, Rosie shifted her feet, and then she squatted and put her hand down against the ground. She gathered her magic in an instant, and then used it to slowly spread the water out so it wouldn't drown the root system of the grass in the one spot.

Nearby, Gabriel came to watch. "What're you doing?" he finally asked.

Rosie looked up at him, and then gestured for him to come closer. "Scoot down and put your hand here next to mine," she said, trying not to feel at least a little bit amused at his hesitation. But he did it. When his hand was nestled in the grass next to hers, she began to slowly release her magic again.

"You're distributing the water," he said appreciatively.

Rosie nodded. "You just have to do it slowly, to make sure it's even," she said. "Why don't you give it a try?"

His eyes widened. "Really?"

"Really." A gentle smile curved her lips as he shuffled forward eagerly but awkwardly on his haunches, moving to the exact spot she had be working on. "Just sink your fingertips in a little for more control—that's it," she said approvingly as Gabe began to channel his magic into the task with a grace and tenderness that surprised her. The way he was always flicking around his lighter, she would have had him pegged as a natural with destructive magic, but he had a real talent for green magic.

When the task was done, Gabe stood and brushed his earth-stained hand down the front of his soggy shorts. "Thanks for showing me that," he said, the words sounding every bit as awkward to say as he must have found them.

"You're welcome," Rosie said, her smile still in place.

Gabe passed Declan on the porch steps—the younger making for the house, the elder making his way to her. As he approached, he fixed her with an expression that was one part pleased, one part proud, and one part still playful. He held his hand out to her, in order to help her up from the lawn.

"My lady."

STEPPING INTO THE SHOWER HAD NEVER FELT BETTER IN her entire *life*. Rosie immediately lathered herself in soap and scrubbed shampoo into her hair, which she then began to hastily wash out with a view to a repeat performance. A stinging sensation in her eye made her curse, and she reached up to soothe the sensation with her fingertips when she heard the lock on the bathroom door click open. A thrill of panic shot through her. Rosie's hands shot out to cover herself and she tried to open one of her squinty eyes to see who was coming in, but that just let more soap in.

She felt Declan's aura long before he opened the

ancient metal-paned shower door to let himself in with her. Rosie backed up blindly to give him room, pressing her fingers back to her stinging eyes. After a few moments of vigorous scrubbing sounds, she felt Declan's hand on her waist.

"Here," he said gently, handing her a wash-cloth. She accepted it gratefully, dabbing her eyes until the pain started to ease.

"Declan," she began, her voice sounding hollow in the steamy, tiled room.

"Shh," he murmured, reaching for the soap.

She opened her eyes in time to see him building a thick lather, focusing intently. Rosie thought to protest —being splattered with dog crap didn't exactly get her motor running—but it didn't seem like his mind was on sex, either. He began to wash her arms with smooth, circular motions, working his way up to her shoulders. He kneaded her sore, tired neck with his strong fingers, and she couldn't help but sigh with pleasure and relief.

Working two jobs was taking its toll, let alone being a mom to Maggie. The trouble with Gabe on top of it all was the icing on the cake. But Declan seemed to know exactly where to press to help all of that momentarily melt away. He gripped her shoulders and turned her, working between her shoulder-blades and along her spine. And then, just when she thought he had finished, he began to shampoo her hair.

His fingertips gave just the right amount of pressure on her scalp, and the way he let them trail through her long tresses was nothing short of heavenly. Rosie let her head loll back as he guided her under the water to rinse, before he conditioned for her as well. She felt like she might be dreaming, it felt that good, but his voice in her ear brought her back to the land of the lucid.

"Sorry I covered you in dog shit," he murmured.

Rosie thought about it for a moment, but then the sight of Declan swatting the broom down and then leaning over the porch rail suddenly tickled her sense of humor. She pressed her lips together, but the laugh refused to back down. It burst out of her mouth like the start of a raspberry, and before she knew it she was giggling in the shower, leaning back against Declan for support. He had started laughing too, the sound deep in his broad chest as he wrapped his arms protectively around her waist.

After a few moments Rosie turned in his arms, the mirthful expression simmering as she looked up into his handsome face. He glanced down his nose at her, water streaming from his beard, where silvery hairs were definitely starting to show among the rust-colored ones. She was suddenly reminded of a certain Grey wizard from a certain fantasy franchise, and she started to giggle again, but he lifted his hand and tilted her chin up so that he could kiss her instead.

The bathroom was still deliciously steamy as Declan and Rosie dried themselves and got dressed for bed. Rosie bent forward so that she could dry her hair, Rosie squeezed her dark locks and thought about what the heck they were going to do, moving forward. Gabe obviously hadn't been directly involved in the poop attack, but she had no doubt that someone he *knew* had.

"You know," she said in a low but conversational tone, not wanting her voice to carry with the bathroom acoustics or sound overly serious. "Between us, I'm sure we can come up with a plan."

"A pwan?" Declan asked around his toothbrush.

Rosie gave her hair one more scrub with the towel for good measure, and then flipped the right way back up. "A plan," she reiterated, rolling her eyes at the wall the bathroom shared with the living room.

Realization dawned on Declan's face. "Ahh," he acknowledged, minty foam gathering at the corner of his mouth. He leaned forward to spit it out. "A plan'd be grand," he said, pausing to smile briefly at his rhyme, "but where do we even start?"

Rosie hung up her towel and reached for a comb instead. "A curfew, for starters," she said, raising a brow and dipping her head in reference to Gabe's late hours and refusal to come home one night at all. "Some actual ground rules wouldn't go astray, either."

"Maybe we can make a list of chores to be done around the Cottage," Declan suggested, turning to lean against the basin swathed in his towel.

"We definitely need to be able to keep a better eye on him," Rosie agreed. "If only we could get one of those police ankle monitors," she half joked.

Declan brightened, and for a moment Rosie thought he was going to say he knew a guy. "What about if he worked with you at Nourish for the summer—for free," he added. "It also means he's off the streets for a large part of the day."

Rosie nodded thoughtfully. "That a great idea, but it would need to be half Nourish, and half delivery rounds with you. We still have Maggie all summer too, don't forget."

"We'll work out some kind of roster," Declan said, nodding thoughtfully. "Maybe we can switch out days where one is with me, and one is with you. That way they'll still have weekends with their friends."

"And we'll get a break," Rosie said emphatically.

"We'll need it," Declan sighed. "What else should we do?"

Rosie shrugged, stepping into her pyjamas. "Just... watch him like a hawk."

Declan allowed himself a small, humorless chuckle. "Easier said than done."

"Not if we're determined," Rosie pointed out. "We're witches, remember?"

At that, the remnant of Declan's chuckle became a slow, deliberate grin.

"We're gonna rock this," he promised.

A few minutes later while Declan was outside modifying the wards that kept Fox Cottage safe, Rosie slipped into the quiet darkness of their bedroom. She left the light off as she drifted over the bedroom window, drawing back the drapes. It wasn't quite a full moon, but it was certainly getting there. The whole front lawn was illuminated, and moonbeams highlighted the huge, majestic oak tree in the front yard.

Pressing her palms against the glass, Rosie pushed her magical energy out towards the oak tree that had stood watch over Fox Cottage and its inhabitants for centuries.

"If we've ever needed a watchful eye for trouble, it's now," she said determinedly. The leaves on the tree seemed to shimmer before they had a burst of incandescent light pulse over them; a sign that the tree had accepted Rosie's request for aid. She let her hands stay against the glass a moment longer then opened the window. The warm summer breeze rushed into the room, soothing Rosie as she slipped into bed to wait for Declan, safe in the knowledge that the oak tree would alert her to anyone sneaking about where they had no business being.

CHAPTER NINE

"Here, Mom," Maggie said, placing a plate of hot buttered toast in front of Rosie as she sat down at the kitchen table the next morning. Rosie felt her heart go as soft and gooey as that butter.

"Aww! Thanks hon," she said, beaming. "That's so sweet of you."

Maggie puffed her chest out a little. She bustled back into the kitchen just as Declan and Gabe emerged. Their hair might have been different shades, but they both had the exact same type of bed-head. Gabe was running his fingers through his and managed to tame it into a trendy mop in a matter of seconds, his attention caught by the action in the kitchen. Rosie *wished* her hair was that easy to control.

"I'm making you guys some now," Maggie promised, putting another four slices of bread into the toaster.

"You're an angel," Declan declared in a dramatic voice that made Maggie grin. "Ya make the best toast I've ever had, an' I don't mind sayin' it," he added, pouring two cups of coffee. He handed one to Rosie and sat down as Gabe reached for the carton of orange juice on the table.

"Thanks, Mags," he said, quite possibly the politest thing he'd said to anyone in the house since he'd been there. Rosie glanced at Declan. She didn't know when exactly they were going to be having their conversation with Gabriel about his new rules, but she bet it would change Gabe's suddenly positive attitude.

"What are you gonna do at work today?" Maggie asked Rosie conversationally, readying two extra plates while Gabe scrolled through his phone.

"Well actually," Rosie said, catching Declan's eye to give him the heads up that she was steering this ship into uncharted waters. "Declan and I wanted to talk to you two about that."

Gabe didn't look up but his thumb paused, hovering over his screen. Still fresh from the egg-cleaning incident, Maggie looked at her mother warily. "How come?"

"The summer's a long time," Declan chimed in. "So your mum and I thought that it would be a good idea for you kids to spend some time working with each of us."

"Yeah!" Maggie agreed, brightening. "Mom already talked to me about working at Nourish with her, some days!"

"That's right," Rosie nodded. "But some days you'll be helping Declan with his deliveries, too."

Maggie eyed Declan speculatively. "Can we listen to my favorite podcast in the truck?"

Declan eyed her back just as speculatively. "Okay," he agreed. "But only if ya go and see to all your greenhouse chores right now, before we all start our day."

"Cool!" Feeling like she won the round, Maggie skipped out to make good on her end of the bargain.

"Here we go," Gabe sighed, flicking an app closed.

"Gabe, ya have to know that your behavior's been well below unacceptable," Declan said, angling his body towards his teenage son. "We all have to try t'get along."

"We wouldn't need to get along if you'd just sign my emancipation forms," Gabe reminded him. "I'd be halfway back to London by now."

Things weren't exactly going according to plan. Declan looked to Rosie for an assist. She straightened, prepared to play Bad Cop.

"Well he's not ready to make that decision," she supplied diplomatically, earning herself a grateful nod from Declan. "And you're going to be here with us for the next little while, at least. So with that in mind, there are some new rules that you're going to need to follow."

Gabe looked from her to his father. Rosie took the opportunity to look from Declan to *Gabe*, gesturing to Declan with her eyes and a quick jutting of her chin in the boy's direction.

"Like what?" Gabe asked, bored.

"Like you're going to be home by no later than 9pm each night," Declan said, sitting up a little taller in his chair. "Telling us where you're going, and not going to any place that isn't where you're meant to be without checking with us first."

"This is ridiculous," Gabe said, letting his head fall back as he focused his attention on the kitchen ceiling. "I'm not a baby. I didn't even have any of these dumb rules back home."

"We have rules because we care about you," Declan told him, "so you'll be followin' them, dumb or not."

Rosie stepped in to back him up. "That's right. You also will be asking permission before you stay the night at anyone else's house, you won't be staying at the house of anyone whose parents we don't know, and we will need contact information for their parents."

"And no drinkin', smokin', or law breakin'," Declan added jabbing an index finger of warning in Gabe's direction. "Or secrets. From now on."

'So your plan," Gabe said slowly, "is to suffocate me and make me look dumb in front of my friends?"

"We're sorry if you feel suffocated," Rosie said, "but the rules are here to stay. How you look in front of your friends depends on how you choose to react to them."

Pushing back in his chair, Gabe folded his arms over his chest and glared across the table at them both. "Sure," he said, the lightness of his voice a stark contrast to the resentment in his sea-green eyes. "Whatever you guys say."

THE NEXT FEW DAYS PASSED IN A BLUR OF SLEEPLESS nights and hectic days. Declan, who had taken to sleeping on the porch swing out on the lawn as an extra line of defence against wily teenage boys. He was woken up at 2am by Gabe getting tangled in magic Rosie had asked the oak tree to perform as he was trying to sneak out. The next day Gabe 'accidentally' dropped a tray full of plates while he was busing tables at Nourish, and then vanished at the end of his shift only to be found hours later down by the waterfront with his friends.

Personally, Rosie would like to meet the person who penned the term 'rules were made to be broken' just so she could tell them in no uncertain terms what she thought about their philosophy.

By the time Thursday rolled around, Rosie and Declan were both exhausted trying to keep up with Gabe's ability to get around all of their rules and punishments. Rosie yawned as she walked down street to Nourish, a cup from home clutched in her hand but not quite doing the job of waking her up.

She wandered past the ice creamery and the farmer's market, cutting across the playground she sometimes visited with Maggie as she moved towards the park. A crowd of people were gathered around the General Beaufort Moss Memorial Fountain that sat on the corner. She personally thought that the fountain—with General Moss seated arrogantly on the back of his rearing steed—was way too over-the-top. Rosie idly wondered if there was some kind of local holiday today that she hadn't been aware of and made a mental note to ask Tammy about it later on. But then she cancelled that thought as she realized *exactly* why the crowd had gathered.

Someone had filled the fountain with detergent. Bubbles were shooting high in the air, carried off by the light morning breeze. As she got closer Rosie could see that the foam had overflowed the fountain itself and was oozing between the feet of the onlookers, dribbling down the sidewalk and into the stormwater drain. She almost laughed—it seemed like a harmless prank—until reality hit her.

Freakin' Gabriel Forrest.

Rosie hurried forward, clutching her coffee cup for dear life as she wriggled her way through the crowd to assess the damage. When she finally managed to get past Earl from the Post office (who was artfully hiding a smirk) and Grace Simmons the ex-school principal (who looked utterly scandalized), Rosie saw that the situation was much, *much* worse than she had first imagined.

Proud ol' General Moss was dressed to the nines in lingerie.

Her lingerie.

Her mouth fell open with shock and anger as she noticed her best garnet-colored bra draped over his puffed-out chest, the matching panties cut and then stapled back together over his britches. A sparkly white feather boa was draped around his neck, sodden from the bubbles that continued to sprout obscenely over the whole scene. His noble steed was momentarily blinded by another bra—not hers—this one incandescently white with dozens of white beaded crosses embroidered onto the cups. The *piece de resistance* was that the horse was wearing the sparkly matching thong, which had been artfully stretched so that the pearl cross that made up the actual thong string was fully intact.

"Well!" Beverly huffed, "in addition to the obvious vulgarity, I'm *horrified* that we have women in this town who are so blasphemous!"

A snort of laughter finally escaped Earl, who buckled it in when Beverly fixed him with a sternly disapproving glare.

Out of the corner of her eye, she caught another person staring up at the statue in horrified profile. Prissy Bishop held one hand up to her temple as though blocking anyone from seeing her reaction, but she wasn't doing a very good job. Almost as though she sensed Rosie's attention on her Prissy wheeled around, her eyes narrowing as they met Rosie's gaze.

She marched over through the crowd and then leaned over her crossed arms to hiss venomously at Rosie.

"I hope you're *happy*," she snapped.

Rosie's brows knitted in confusion, but then released themselves in understanding. Apparently *Prissy* was the hussy who wore blasphemous undergarments.

"This would never have happened if it wasn't for that delinquent of yours," she stage-whispered. "My boy wouldn't do something like this on his *own*."

Rosie lifted her chin. "Really?" she spat back. "Because that's not what I heard."

Prissy's face flattened and then scrunched up in another sneer. "Well, it's good to know that Mosswood's pastor speaks so freely of our son's personal difficulties. I'm sure our custody mediator will be very glad to know how little he values Matthew's privacy."

Rosie felt all the blood leave her face. Prissy noticed, too, and her gaze darted smugly around Rosie's face. She leaned forward an inch more.

'Keep that no-good little *heathen* away from my son."

Rosie stood up to her full height rather than letting Prissy push her backwards, and she crossed her own arms.

"And you keep your mouthy little hypocrite away from *mine*."

Prissy's jaw muscle clenched and then released. She turned on her heel and marched along the cobblestones away from the city center. Rosie looked around and saw people noticing them. She gripped her coffee tighter and gave the newly-fashionable Beaufort Moss one more glance before leaving the square herself.

Her mind turned over and over one word in her exchange with Prissy which had surprised Rosie most. She had called Gabriel *mine*.

SHE THOUGHT SHE WAS HOME FREE WHEN SHE MADE IT halfway up Lee Street without seeing any further carnage, until she heard someone shout her name from behind her. A glance over her shoulder revealed Maude Merriweather huffing and puffing to catch up with her. Rosie stopped to wait, wishing that Maude had chosen literally any other time to want to chat. She loved the older woman. Maude was tenacious, didn't mince words, and had more of a 'kick-ass aunt' vibe than motherly tendencies. But she was really not in the mood.

"Rosie," Maude gasped as she hurried up to her. "I'm—so—glad—to—"

"Hold up," Rosie said, finding her kindness. She placed a hand on the plump, short woman's shoulder to steady her. The last thing she needed was Maude having a heart attack. "Catch your breath first."

Maude threw her a grateful look, sucked in a few long, healthy breaths, and then tried again. "The Dames," she huffed. "They're gone! I looked everywhere I could think of," she took another deep breath, "but I can't find a trace of 'em!"

Rosie blinked, mystified. "Did you check with Veronica at the vet clinic? Maybe she—"

Maude shook her head emphatically. "No, she wouldn't take 'em without tellin' me—and she's not seen so much as a feather!"

Keenly aware that opening time for Nourish was pretty much *now*, Rosie guided Maude forward gently. "Why don't you come on up to Nourish with me? I've got to open up, but then I'll make you a cup of tea and we can do some ringin' around, okay?"

"Thank you," Maude wheezed gratefully.

The pair of them made the journey past the Town Hall at Maude's pace, which was about a third of Rosie's. They turned into the laneway and moseyed over to Nourish which was almost on the corner.

"Now don't you fret," Rosie told Maude, slipping her key into the lock and reaching inside to flip the CLOSED sign over so that it said OPEN. "I'm sure that the Dames can't have gotten far. "Maybe they—"

The door opened with the tinkling of the usual bell that announced to Tammy and Rosie they had customers, but this time it was accompanied by a loud and indignant 'BUK-KERK!'.

A fluffy-feathered hen flapped her wings, annoyed to be disturbed, as she took off at a scurry across the polished wood flooring of Nourish's dining room.

"Arlene!" Maude exclaimed, her tone full of relief

and confusion. "What n God's green earth are you doin' *here*, missy!?"

And then Maude and Rosie took in the rest of the dining room.

There were chickens *everywhere*. They were huddled together on tables, roosting in her house plants, and scratching the top of the service counter. One particularly adventurous hen had managed to get itself up onto an exposed metal beam high above the dining area, the egg it had laid balanced precariously on the edge. Rosie blinked repeatedly as she surveyed the situation, hoping each time that she was hallucinating only to see the same horrific scene each time she re-opened her eyes.

But worse than the hens themselves was the mess. Feathers of every hue were scattered across the tables and floor, perfectly complimenting the chicken poop that was splattered everywhere too. It took Rosie all of three seconds to link the dog poop, and the fountain, and the hens. She felt her face getting hot, her anger reaching boiling point.

Maude wasn't a stupid woman, by any means. She was shrewd and astute, and she noticed Rosie's hesitance with the wisdom of a woman who was about to pick her next words carefully.

"I'm not usually one for puns," she said, looking around the room. "But seems to me, Rosie Bell, you've got some trouble in your henhouse."

Gentle clucking surrounded Rosie once Maude was

gone. She flipped the sign back to CLOSED just as the hot sting of tears flooded her eyes.

"AND YOU'RE *SURE* YOU DIDN'T GET ANY KIND OF message from 'im?"

Declan was looking at Rosie expectantly across the kitchen table at Fox Cottage, as though maybe she had been holding out on him all night. It was hours since dinner—an event that Gabe had neglected to show up for—and his curfew had been and gone.

"No messages," she reiterated, the answer compounding the tightness she was feeling across her chest. "Nothing."

"What the bloody hell does he think he's playin' at?"

"I don't know what to think anymore," Rosie sighed, pressing her fingertip down onto some crumbs that covered the top of the table. "Except that his antics are hurting our family and our friends. And now they're hurting my *business*." She pressed her lips together, willing herself not to cry. "I used magic to clean up most of the mess the Dames left, but it still took Tammy and I the rest of the day to get it spick and span! Thank goodness the health inspector didn't make an unscheduled visit while our dining room was full of chicken shit!"

Declan slid his hand across the table to cover hers,

momentarily stilling her nervous fingers. "I'm sorry, Rosie."

She glanced at him; her unconventionally handsome boyfriend who melted her heart with his roguish charm. But that charm was nowhere to be seen. It had been bled from him, leaving sadness and uncertainty in his eyes, and it broke her heart to see it. She could blame him and his lack of parenting know-how all she wanted, but this all boiled down to being the fault of one single person. And that person hadn't even bothered to show up to face the music.

"Me too," she murmured, her lips tightening into a humorless smile that probably wasn't as bolstering as she'd hoped it would be.

"Are we doin' the right thing here?" Declan asked suddenly, looking into the middle-distance. "Maybe this just... isn't working."

Rosie studied his face for a moment, narrowing her eyes a little when she found that she couldn't make out what he was asking.

"That depends," she said. "Are we talking about the rules, or are we talking about something... bigger?"

"I don't know," Declan admitted quietly, resting his forehead on the palm of his hand.

They sat like that—heads resting on the table, holding hands, faces turned towards each other—and the clock ticked away the hours. The house was silent, Maggie long since having been in bed. Declan was gently snoring and Rosie was just starting to doze, her thoughts about how sore her neck was going to be in the morning starting to fade into slumber.

Declan's phone blared into life, the dulcet tones of the Snow Patrol song he used as his ringtone ripping them both back to the present moment with electrifying precision. They both scrambled to sit and he lunged to snatch up his phone and put it on speaker.

"Hello?"

"Mr. Forrest?" The voice on the end was cool and no-nonsense.

"Yes," he said hesitantly, his brows tilting down as he fixed Rosie with a worried look.

"This is Sheriff Star. We have your son Gabriel here."

Oh my God. Rosie leapt to her feet, pushing her chair back with a squeak of protest from the floor. He was at the Sheriff's Department? The air inside the balloon of tension inside of her had expanded to maximum capacity. It was about to burst, and she didn't know what she could do to stop it.

"Is he alright?" Declan asked, his voice sounding as tight as his white-knuckled grip on his phone.

"Well," the Sheriff replied curtly. "He's not physically injured."

Declan let out an explosive breath of relief. "Thank you."

"Mmhmm," The Sheriff added, sounding unimpressed as she carried on. "I'm calling to let you know that Gabriel is being held for questioning. We can't question him without the consent of his parent or guardian. Do you consent to the questioning, Mr. Forrest?"

Rosie's head felt like it was in a spin. She was having flashbacks to her own experiences with Sheriff Larry Holt last Christmas, remembering the bleakness of the holding cells she'd been forced into at the Sheriff's Department. She was thinking back to what she'd always done any time she'd needed to bail Randy out of jail, and what the process had been like in terms of keeping him out of the firing line.

"Questioning?" Declan stiffened, his eyes meeting Rosie's. "For what?"

"Gabriel is being held on suspicion of grand theft auto and destruction of property."

"What?!" Declan exclaimed.

Rosie grabbed his upper arm, squeezing slightly to get his attention.

"Tell her that you don't consent to him being questioned without you being present," she said. If nothing else, that would buy them some time. She thought she remembered Ben saying he had a lawyer; maybe she could get the name from him.

Declan nodded, before speaking back into the phone. "I don't consent—"

"Thanks," Sheriff Star said wryly. "I heard. Alright. Please make your way down to the Department when you can."

She terminated the call, and Declan and Rosie were

left to stare at each other across the wasteland of the kitchen table.

"What the hell has he done," Declan asked rhetorically, shell-shocked.

"*Now*," Rosie added, ready to burst. "What has he done *now?*"

CHAPTER TEN

Declan's truck coasted onto Mosswood's Main Street. Rosie could see the lights before she saw anything else: blue and red flashes relentlessly warning of danger. A fire department truck was pulled up hastily on the wrong side of the street to block traffic one-way, and an officer from the Sheriff's Department waved Declan through the bottleneck.

Prissy Bishop's pristine, pearly white SUV was sticking out of the front of the Go-Go Mart, the back tires off the ground entirely. There was shattered glass all over the road, the front of the vehicle was totaled, and something oozed ominously out from underneath the engine bay. A fire hydrant was bent out of shape gushing water all over the scene.

The inside of the store looked like a war-zone. The magazine racks had all splintered and displays of last-minute-purchase items had been decimated. Packets of pork rinds and peanuts littered the floor, along with gum, candy bars, and a bunch of other stuff. The front of the car had wound up hitting the actual service counter, which had been pushed over until it crashed, leaving a huge gaping hole in the drywall.

"Oh no..." Rosie breathed, craning her neck to survey the damage as they passed. She felt physically sick seeing this kind of carnage and was grateful that Carol-Ann had agreed to go and stay at the house with Maggie while she slept. Despite everything she was glad to know that Gabe was physically unharmed... but what about Ben? Had he been *serving* someone when that car had hit that counter?

Goosebumps broke out all over Rosie, and she braced herself with one hand on the dash of the truck for a second as she tried to get ahold of her breathing and the dizzy feeling that threatened to overcome her.

"Jesus," Declan groaned under his breath, pulling the truck into a parking space out front of the Sheriff's Department across the street.

Declan popped the door open from the outside, and it helped to snap Rosie out of it. She shook her head to clear it before sliding down onto the sidewalk, Declan holding her hand firmly as they marched up the slight ramp and into the Sheriff's Department foyer. They were immediately greeted by faux walnut wood panel-ing, and strange, teal-colored linoleum. A huge potted palm hulked in one corner like an overprotective security guard, and underneath it was a man hunched over with his head in his hands.

"Ben!" Rosie cried, dropping Declan's hand and rushing over to her friend. "Oh my gosh—Are you *alright?"*

Ben looked up at the sound of his name, a wan smile creeping onto his boyishly charming face when he saw Rosie. He had bags under his eyes as though he'd just had ten years of life scared out of him, and he looked like he could use a stiff drink. Rosie was overwhelmed with happiness and relief to see that he was in one piece and flung her arms around his neck before he could protest, squeezing tightly.

"Yeah," he grunted under the weight of her forceful hug before she released him. "Nobody was hurt, at least. I was just about to lock up when it happened. I had some paperwork to finish, else this could've turned out a little worse for me. Hey man," he added to Declan, who stepped up to give him a rough, brotherly hug of his own.

"We're so glad you're okay," Declan said, his voice tinged with undercurrents of guilt and apology.

"Thanks," Ben said with a crooked, relieved smile. "Me too. I'm glad we all are." He nodded his head at the glass interview room that was just off the foyer—the one usually reserved for people who needed to make statements, or who wanted to try and sweet-talk the Sheriff out of a parking ticket. Gabe and Matthew were seated next to each other at the round table. Neither of them were speaking, and they both looked like they were auditioning for the role of Tough Guy #1 on Law and Order.

Before anyone could stop him, Declan steam-rolled his way through the door, making both boys jump in the process.

"What have you got to say for yourself?" he demanded. A muscle ticked in his jaw as he glared at Gabriel, leaning on the table the pair of boys sat behind.

After he recovered from the initial shock of seeing his father looming in the doorway, Gabe's attention darted back to Matthew. He rolled his shoulders back and hunched down in his seat a little, as though trying to come across like a kid who was used to being in and out of police stations.

When no answer came, Declan spoke again. "This isn't good enough, Gabriel," he warned.

"I don't care whether you think it's good enough or not," Gabe snapped. "The only thing mum wanted from you was your blood, and neither of you wanted me."

"I know," Declan sighed, almost as though he had been waiting for those words to fall from Gabriel's lips.

"Whatever," was all that Gabe replied. He crossed one arm over his chest and flicked his lighter open. He stared into the flame instead of looking at his father.

Rosie's chin sank at the exchange. But she was then distracted by a shiny red sedan screeching to a halt right outside the Sheriff's Department. The passenger door was flung open, and Prissy Bishop flew up the ramp and into the foyer like a rabid harpy.

"Where is he?" she demanded dramatically as soon as she entered the building. "Where is my son?"

Myles opened his mouth to answer, but Prissy cut him off. Spotting Rosie, she turned and crossed her arms, one hip jutting out. "I told you your son was a troublemaker."

Rosie felt her expression steel over. "Well, at least he never stole my car."

Prissy opened her mouth to respond but was interrupted when Sheriff Star emerged from the hallway that, Rosie knew from unfortunate experience, led to the holding cells. As the Sheriff greeted the new arrival, Rosie felt Declan's gaze on her. She looked over to meet his eyes, and he straightened his lips. He reached for her hand and squeezed. Rosie glanced down at their joined hands, not entirely sure she deserved the gratitude she saw shining in his eyes.

"Parents and guardians," the Sheriff said, face stony. "Right this way."

ROSIE AND BEN KEPT QUIET COMPANY WITH EACH OTHER while the necessary proceedings took place. Rosie hadn't been invited to go in, and in a way she was relieved. She was so mad at Gabe that she didn't know if she could stand to listen to his attitude and being closer to Prissy in that moment might just be the straw that broke the camel's back. She sighed and leaned back against the hard plastic chair, trying to get comfortable and failing miserably.

A little while later, the door of the ancient but functional automatic door to the lobby whooshed open and Tammy clicked in wearing tasteful heels and a worried expression.

"Thank the good Lord you're alright!" were the first words out of her mouth as she rushed forward to kiss Ben on the cheek with sisterly relief. "I just about had kittens when Myles told me what happened! Where are they?"

"Being interviewed," Rosie supplied. She shifted her weight, unsure what kind of reaction she would get from Tammy, but all Tammy did was nod.

"Just as well," she said, "the sooner this mess is sorted out the better. I'm just glad that no one was injured." She barely took a breath before she dug into the bag she was carrying. "Here. I brought y'all something to eat." She held out brown paper bags to each of them. Ben eagerly reached for one, but Rosie politely shook her head at the other. Tammy sat down and rolled the bag up into her lap.

"That's real sweet of you," Ben said as he grabbed out a sandwich rolled up into parchment paper. "It's been a helluva night."

The room fell back into an awkward silence as Ben bit into his sandwich. The only sounds in the room were those of Ben munching on his belated dinner. Tammy was the first to speak.

"Do you… have insurance, Ben?" she asked.

Ben glanced up at Tammy and then at Rosie and then back to his sandwich. He cleared his throat before he spoke. His next words were measured, as though he'd been weighing them and only just now had the chance to let them sink into the conversation.

"Well, I'd be lyin' if I told you I wasn't worried about the impact this is gonna have on me financially," he said, worrying at the back of his neck with his hand. A notoriously private person in town, Ben was something of a mystery to the gossips of Mosswood. Rosie didn't know anything about the Go-Go's financial situation, but if Ben was rich then he didn't show it. He was a modest kind of guy who had modest kinds of tastes— from his wood-paneled station wagon right through to the tiny one-bedroom apartment that he lived in right above the store.

"I don't know when I'm going to be able to open the store again—those kinds of repairs could take months, and the summer money is what carries me through most of the rest of the year." He hesitated, before adding, "and the insurance company is going to want copies of the police report."

Her heart sank. The subtext was that he might have to press charges to get his insurance company to pay for the repairs he needed. Rosie chewed the inside of her cheek, trying to find the words she needed.

She stared down at her own hands as her friends spoke around her. Their words settled unhappily into the cracks caused by the unease she had been feeling around Tammy, Myles, and Maude lately. It was the same sensation Rosie had felt growing steadily in all her relationships—like a virus gaining hold. It seemed like she was running out of places where her household would feel welcome, and the thought of losing the local family she had come to love and depend on so much over the past year was enough make her eyes sting with the threat of tears.

But Declan, Myles, Prissy, and their wayward sons emerged from wherever it was they had gone and Rosie was grateful for the distraction no matter how long it'd taken to present itself. The three in the waiting room stood, and the next few minutes passed in a blur of recited bail conditions and the handing over of credit cards. The truck was silent all the way back to Fox Cottage, Rosie's head full of what Ben had begrudgingly said and the fact that Declan was now five thousand dollars worth of bail bond lighter.

BY THE TIME THE WHOLE HOUSEHOLD WAS IN BED, Rosie knew she wouldn't be able to get a wink of sleep. She lay awake in the darkness, feeling the warmth of Declan by her side and wondering if he was drifting off or just as awake as she was. She bit the inside of her bottom lip and hesitated, before barely whispering "Are you awake?"

She heard his head turn towards her. "Course I'm awake," he sighed, sounding ten years older than his usual happy-go-lucky self. Rosie shuffled closer to him, slipping her arm around his middle and threading her fingers into his. He brushed his fingertips over hers.

"I was worried you wouldn't have the money to bail him out," she admitted. "It's such a huge amount. I half wonder if the Sheriff didn't hope you wouldn't be able to afford it."

"I can't," he admitted hoarsely. "That was more than I had in my savings—and the credit card will only get me through until the repayment is due next month." He paused a beat, and then sounded resigned. "I'm gonna have to ask me Da' for some money."

Rosie pressed her eyes closed in sadness and frustration. "I'm sorry." She wriggled a little closer, as though hoping to be able to provide comfort by proximity.

"That's not even the worst of it," he continued, sounding more agitated. "What if he goes to jail? What if they send him back to England? I'm supposed to be lookin' after him, and not a month later he's in bloody jail."

Rosie sighed. She didn't have all the answers—hell, at this point she'd settle for just one. But with all the other things coming around, she kept coming back to one sad thought.

"Maybe his going back to England wouldn't have to

be such a bad thing," she suggested gently. "You'd think he would've had *some* kind of stability there for the last fourteen years."

"Yeah, because Gemma was so stable," he snapped, disconnecting his hand from hers. "Is that really the only solution you can see to this problem? Sending him away?"

Rosie half sat up, frowning. "Of course that's not—"

"Maybe I should just go back across the pond with him," Declan cut her off, shifting away from her and sitting up himself. "Then you could have all the peace and quiet you want!"

"Hey," Rosie countered, her voice steady and true. "That's not what I meant, and you know it." Rosie took a deep breath and then decided to stop overthinking this. She needed to speak from her heart.

"I think that Gabe is acting out because he doesn't *know* you—or Maggie or me. His whole world has been turned upside down," she said, taking Declan's hand back. He didn't pull away from her, but he wasn't exactly reciprocating either. It was a backslide from their intimate interlude in the shower, and Rosie felt like her heart was so bruised by everything that she didn't know if it would repair or rot away.

"He doesn't know where his mom is," she pointed out, "and he has to be worried about that. He's only just met his father and he's in an entirely different country. That's a *lot* of change for one kid." She squeezed Declan's hand for emphasis. "I only meant that being back on his home turf might make it easier for him to adjust to all the rest."

"Yeah," Declan huffed. "And it's my fault, Rosie. It's my fault he was born and it's my fault his mum is gone. How do I make that up to him?"

She squeezed his hand again just before he pulled away from her a second time, lying down on his side facing away from her.

"I just want to do right by him. I have to."

If there was one thing about this whole mess that Rosie could understand, it was *that*. Being a parent—no matter how long the term of office—was a harrowing experience filled with laughter, joy, constant anxiety, and more love than you could poke a stick at. There was no 'off' switch, and she had spent her fair share of sleepless nights worrying about Maggie and their situation to know that Declan's attempt to look as though he wanted to sleep was more about needing head space than anything else.

"I know," she replied gently. She let her gaze trace the outline of Declan's head in the darkness, following the outer shell of his ear down to his jaw before up the sweeping curve of his neck towards his shoulder. There was no response from him so she held back the sigh she dearly wished to release and laid down herself, their backs to one another as though a whole ocean stretched between them.

CHAPTER ELEVEN

Dinners around the kitchen table at Fox Cottage had come to feel like a three-ring circus with Rosie as the reluctant Ringmaster. In one ring off to the side, her relationship with Declan was balancing spinning plates on flexible sticks. They turned faster and faster, and the very real threat of breaking more plates than they could catch between them was starting to make Rosie sweat. The other side ring was playing host to the juggling act she was orchestrating with all their friends, trying to keep everyone happy and in the air at the same time while also walking an obstacle course set out for her by Gabe.

And right there in the center ring was the main event: The Failing Family Unit. Step right up folks, and watch the disaster unfold right before your very eyes! No safety net, no wires—just pure adrenaline and death-defying stunts that was sure to have everyone on the edges of their seat all the way through a healthy serving of steak, potato salad, and collard greens.

It felt like everyone was holding their breath and waiting for the free-fall.

"How is reading camp going?"

Rosie wasn't surprised that Gabe was the one to break the silence. In fact, she had pretty much expected it. Gabe liked pushing people's buttons, and this was the only button in the room to push. She glanced at Declan, who raised a brow ever-so-slightly.

Maggie looked surprised that Gabe had spoken to her at all. She swallowed her mouthful of steak, shrugging.

"It's okay, I guess," she said. "But Allalyn keeps taking the next book in my series so I have to wait to read it. She's so annoying."

Gabe's nose wrinkled, one corner of his mouth tugging downwards in an annoyed frown. "Dumb name," he declared. "Maybe you can do the same thing back to her," he advised, spearing a piece of potato with his fork. "Take the next book after that."

"But then I wouldn't know what was going on," Maggie sighed, digging around in her greens. "Because I wouldn't have read the book in between."

"Okay," he shrugged. "I'll take you to the library so you can get the book in between."

Rosie laid her fork to one side. "You can't leave the house because you're grounded." She turned her attention to Maggie. "I'll speak to your teacher," she added, reaching for her glass of water.

There was a clatter of cutlery as Gabe abandoned his completely. He pushed up out of his chair roughly, wobbling the table so that all the drinks shivered in fear. Everyone looked up at him—Maggie with surprise, Rosie with warning, and Declan with shock.

"My bad," he snarked at Rosie, green eyes blazing. "I forgot that I wasn't allowed to speak to Maggie without *permission*." He pushed past Maggie's chair, heading straight for the front door.

Rosie blinked and then looked at Declan, who was already laying his cutlery to one side. "I know, I know," he sighed with resignation. "I'll go talk to him." He followed the war-path Gabe had left in his wake.

Rosie laid her knife down next to her fork, leaning forward heavily on the table and pinching the bridge of her nose. She was interrupted by Maggie's sweet, hopeful voice.

"If Gabe's not gonna eat his steak, can I have it?"

THE MORNING SHIFT AT NOURISH THE NEXT DAY PASSED in a blur. Rosie was glad she could operate on autopilot because she was tired of thinking about pretty much *everything*. Coffee and breakfasts and cleaning she could do, and it wasn't until the morning rush was done and dusted that she realized she was almost through her entire shift. When the front door opened with the tinkle of the bell she looked up from giving the coffee machine a wipe over. She had been expecting Tammy, but it wasn't her best friend and business partner who was hastily approaching the counter.

"Myles?" Rosie asked with a concerned frown.

The Pastor looked like he'd been the lightning rod in an electrical storm. His usually carefully styled pompadour was haphazardly windswept, and there was a splash of something that looked suspiciously like coffee—which Myles didn't drink—dribbled down the front of his polo shirt. But most worrisome of all was the wild look in Myles' crystal blue eyes and the pink tinges of color high in his usually pale cheeks. The closer he got, the more Rosie noticed how disheveled he was.

She took a breath. "If you're looking for Tammy, she's—"

"Not lookin' for Tammy," he huffed, as though he had run all the way down the street from the Church. "I... uh. I actually came to see *you.*"

"Me?" Rosie asked incredulously.

"Yes ma'm," he replied. "I need a shoulder, and I can't really talk to Tammy about this... *particular* issue." He looked a little sheepish, but when he spoke there was a note of hope in his tone. "I know things've been kinda strained between us lately, but I figured we're both in the same boat so to speak."

His being there suddenly made sense to Rosie. She

felt flattered that he had sought her out for advice, and grateful that he still counted her a close enough friend to value what she had to say.

"Why don't you have a seat," she told him, making her way out from behind the counter. She crossed the dining room, turned the OPEN sign to CLOSED, and flicked the lock on the door. "Would you like some tea? We have this really great herbal blend, with chamomile and lavender."

A relieved but nervous smile bloomed on Myles' handsome face. "If you're sure it's not too much trouble." He settled himself onto the couch by the counter, his hands clasped primly in his lap. Rosie grabbed a teapot and added the herb mix—one she had put together herself from things she had grown in the garden at Fox Cottage. When she glanced up at Myles, he was looking at her with gratitude written in his brilliantly blue eyes.

"Thank you, Rosie."

"You're welcome any time," she told him, meaning every word.

"Well," he sighed with frustration. "I'm glad *you* think so."

Rosie frowned over the tea setting. "What do you mean?"

He pressed his lips together, looking tortured as he met her gaze through the curling steam that rose from the spout of the teapot. "Just that with all the dust Matthew and Gabriel have been kickin' up, I 'spose I should've known that some of it was bound to get in my eyes sooner or later."

Rosie nodded glumly. "I know what you mean. Doesn't feel like anyone has anything kind to say to me lately that they don't have to force out." She poured the tea, adding a little honey to hers as she heaved a weighty sigh.

"My feelings exactly," Myles agreed, mixing his tea with sugar and a slice of lemon.

Rosie sat back with her mug, taking advantage of the break to put her feet up on the foot stool nearby.

"Why don't you start from the beginning?" she suggested. "We're both in this together. Sometimes just getting it all out can be really helpful."

Myles also sat back in the couch and slouched down until his neck was leaning onto the back cushion.

"So good to be on the receiving end of good advice," he practically moaned with gratitude, making Rosie snort. But as the seconds ticked on, the spark of hope in his eye got duller. The bags under his eyes seemed saggier. And the grip he had on his mug got tighter.

"The truth is..." he drawled, stringing out the words until he eventually had nowhere to go but forwards. "I'm having a hard time letting myself be happy when Matthew's so unhappy."

Rosie had never heard him sounding so defeated, and it made her heart ache a little to see this usually positive beacon at a shadow of his former self. He turned his head against the cushion and looked over, meeting her gaze.

"No doubt you were surprised when I asked Ben to be my best man," he said shyly.

Rosie shrugged lightly. "I *was* a little. I thought you would have asked Matthew, is all."

"I did," Myles told her with a tightly wound frown. "And he flat out refused. Said that he wasn't gonna be party to an *abomination*, and that he wouldn't even be attending."

Rosie felt a small puff of breath leave her. Maggie had pretty much taken to Declan from the very beginning, and after a few hiccups in the early days it had mostly been smooth sailing between them. Sure, they'd had other problems to deal with—but Myles' confession reminded her that it could have all been that much more compounded.

"Oh, wow," she breathed, setting her teacup down. "I'm so sorry. We've been so caught up in the whirlwind on our own side of the fence that we didn't stop to look around and notice the tornado in yours."

"I don't blame you," the pastor smiled sadly. "Y'all have been through a lot since Gabriel arrived. But that fact is that... Well! We have to *face* facts."

He heaved a sigh, and after a moment the full gravity of what he was saying starting seeping through Rosie's layers of feeling one by one, until it finally reached her consciousness.

"But it's tomorrow!" she argued, pulling herself up. "Surely you're not thinking about... *cancelling?*"

"I don't know what I'm thinkin'!" he said quickly, which told Rosie that cancelling the wedding had definitely been on his mind. "Except that I want to make *all* the people I care about happy, and that there's no way to accomplish it. I've been prayin' on it all week, and I still can't see the light!"

Rosie could see she needed to take the steam out of this train before it left the station. "Have you tried talking to Matthew?" she asked pointedly. "About how *you're* feeling?"

"Sure," Myles said, deflating against the couch. He pressed his fingertips to the bridge of his nose and massaged, like it would suddenly rid him of the headache caused by his unruly teenage son. "He's more stubborn than a mule, just like his mother—Lord bless her," Myles added, though Rosie could hear the tension in his tone. He snorted and added "Though she ain't exactly been helpin' matters. In fact, I rather think she's been encouragin' Matthew to stir the pot."

"I don't doubt it," Rosie agreed, the steel in her spine snapping to attention as though drawn by the magnetic power of Prissy's asshattery.

Myles shrugged. "Fact is, it's got me between a rock and hard place. Folks're used to turnin' to *me* in times of crisis as their Pastor, and I'm used to bein' their touchstone whenever something has 'em riled up. But now..."

He trailed off, and Rosie felt her heart squeeze with sympathy for him.

"... You're part of what's got 'em riled," she finished for him quietly.

"Yep," Myles agreed. He looked so hopeless sitting there, like talking to Rosie had momentarily bled him of all the stress and tension but left him empty. "I've heard whispers through the grapevine that there's talk of askin' me to step down."

That news, Rosie thought, was the most shocking of all. From what she had come to learn during her short time in Mosswood, the Church was an absolute institution. There weren't many residents in town who didn't have something to do with it in one way or another, and the pinnacle of that institution was Myles Bishop.

"What?" she asked. She couldn't hide her shock or her concern, but when she saw the look of dejected resignation on Myles' face she sure wished she had've.

"I can't *blame* them, Rosie." He shrugged, failing to look as casual as he was trying to seem. "Maybe I *shouldn't* be the example everyone in Mosswood should be lookin' up to if I can't get through to my own son or keep my own family together."

Rosie conceded, "It's hard. It's emotional, and it's exhausting, and I don't blame you for giving in a little and letting yourself feel it. But I don't think that means you should just give up on everything."

Myles looked over at her as though awaiting the pep talk. Rosie was only too glad to supply it.

"I've never seen two people so well-suited for one another as you and Tammy. People say the Lord works in mysterious ways, but there's nothing mysterious at all about the way you look at each other. He knew what He was doing."

Myles gave in to a small blush at the mention of Tammy, and it was enough to spark hope in Rosie's heart. After taking a couple of moments to consider her words, Myles nodded sagely. It was harder for Rosie to ignore the subtle but uncharacteristic five-o-clock shadow along his jawline when she saw him set it with determination.

"I do believe that's true," he said, "just as I truly believe in my heart that everything happens for a reason. Maybe what the Lord needs to show this town is that helping our neighbors bear their cross is better than nailing them to them."

Rosie smiled at him kindly. "You'll figure it out and set the town to rights again," she promised, "just you wait and see."

He nodded, as though confirming it for himself. "Thanks Rosie. You've given me a lot to think about."

Rosie laughed. "I think you're giving me too much credit. If I had all of the answers," Rosie replied airily, determined to lighten the mood, "then I wouldn't be sailing up the proverbial creek with you, and not a paddle between us."

"Touche," Myles grinned. He paused. "Rosie?"

"Yeah?"

"I haven't told Tammy what I've been thinking," he confessed.

"And she won't hear it from me," Rosie promised.

Relief was the next emotion to flood Myles' handsome but wan face.

"Thank you," he said gratefully.

THE MORNING OF MOSSWOOD'S WEDDING OF THE century had arrived.

Waking up in Tammy's house was so different to waking up at Fox Cottage. For one thing, the sheets were much nicer—they had that buttery soft feeling that hotels seem to magically conjure but which Rosie could never replicate. She stretched in the huge soft bed that she had fallen into the night before, enjoying the sensation for another minute or two before reality set in. Today was the day that her best friend was getting married.

She checked her phone, the same way she did when she woke up every morning, but was surprised to find she had no signal. That was usually more of a problem at Fox Cottage than here in town. With a mental shrug she got out of bed, throwing on her robe and slipping her feet into the fuzzy slippers Tammy had bought for the occasion. They fit perfectly into her Pinterest-worthy surroundings, and Rosie was determined to make the most of the day. And that started with completing her fantasy of descending Tammy's grand staircase on a sunny summer morning feeling every inch like a pampered princess (or in the very least like Scarlet O'Hara).

What she actually descended into was her version of Hell on earth.

Elladine from The Moon Cafe was barking orders at a team of other people from her catering command central in Tammy's kitchen. The oven was in full use, and all types of summery foods were stacked and labelled neatly on the counter ready for morning-tea deployment. There wasn't so much as a whiff of coffee in sight, and Rosie paused on the landing to watch the catering staff dashing around like ants on a chocolate bar.

"Rosie!"

Tammy had caught sight of her, and Rosie turned her head in the direction of the shrill, excited greeting.

Tammy was holding court from what seemed to be a makeshift beauty salon. One woman Rosie had never met was uncurling hot-rollers from Tammy's hair, and another was checking make-up palettes against Tammy's complexion. Tammy herself seemed to be taking it all in her stride and was sitting in a profes-sional-looking black swivel chair with no small degree of pleasure.

"Good afternoon," Tammy teased, gesturing at an identical swivel chair next to hers as Rosie came the rest of the way down the stairs to join her.

Rosie sat reluctantly, trying to keep her feet steadily on the ground to stop the chair from spinning too much. "You shouldn't have let me sleep in," she chided Tammy lightly. "I feel terrible knowing that I was dead to the world while you were down here dealing with all this on your own!"

"I'm not dealin' with anything," Tammy assured her. "I'm sitting here, bein' pampered and drinking champagne. Meet Ellen and Jennifer," she said, introducing the hair and make-up ladies as she handed Rosie a full flute of sparking pale yellow effervescence, topped off with a fresh strawberry. "And now you're bein' pampered too!" Tammy giggled.

"Well," Rosie said, feigning huffiness as she took the glass. "That *does* make me feel a little better about there being no coffee."

"Cheers to that," Tammy agreed, clinking her champagne flute against Rosie's before taking a sip. Her honey-blonde hair was currently falling in soft natural-looking waves over her shoulders, but she soon twisted it into a rough bundle at the nape of her neck. "Up, or down?"

Rosie's brows lifted as she cleared some space on the make-up table's surface. "I thought you would've decided that *weeks* ago,"she said, surprised.

"I thought so too," Tammy sighed, leaning back into her chair, "but apparently choosing wedding hair isn't my strong suit. I was just the same the day I got married to Terry." She said his name softly, as though she hadn't realized that her thoughts were going to lead her to that place. She pressed her lips together and then glanced at Rosie sheepishly through the mirror as Ellen began to tease out her roots to create some volume.

"I dunno why I just mentioned him on today of all days," Tammy said by way of apology. "Talk about the past comin' back to haunt you!"

"Because the last time you made this much of a fuss of yourself was the day you married him?" came Rosie's rhetorical. She fixed Tammy with a sympathetic smile. "It's only natural, hon."

Tammy fell silent, the two women primping with finesse. But when one went to get a particular brush from her car and the other decided she needed a bathroom break, Tammy turned to Rosie with a serious expression on her face.

"Can I ask you a personal question?"

"Of course," Rosie teased lightly. "Doesn't mean I have to feel obliged to answer it."

Tammy flashed a quick grin, before she got serious again. "Were you... *nervous* the first night you and Declan..." She trailed off, her brows lifting as she nodded her head just once to indicate her meaning. Amusement bubbled up inside of Rosie at Tammy's natural way of making everything sound so scandalous. She didn't sugar-coat anything for her friend's benefit.

"The first time I knew I wanted to have sex with Declan, I was so nervous I hardly knew what to do with myself!" she admitted candidly.

"Really?" Tammy asked, almost sighing with relief.

"Of course!" Rosie insisted. "I'd only ever known Randy in that sense, and I guess you could say we'd fallen into a rut during our years together. Or he was so set in the way he did it that I didn't know better," she added bitterly.

"That's me too!" Tammy replied, "with Terry, I mean. I wasn't ever with anyone else, and we did things the Christian way."

Rosie's heart was filled with tenderness for Tammy. She was such a sweet, kind woman. The type of woman who didn't take anything in her life for granted.

"It's good to be a little nervous," she told her sincerely, reaching across the space between them to take Tammy's hand comfortingly. "But don't let it control you," she said.

"Easy for you to say," Tammy said with a dismissive breath of laughter. "You're so confident and gorgeous, and Declan just can't get enough of you." Tammy sighed and reached for her glass. "What if Myles isn't happy with me, once we've said, 'I do'?"

Rosie wasn't going to feed into that kind of insecurity.

"That's the silliest thing I've ever heard you say," she scolded her friend lightly. "*You're* confident and gorgeous, and Myles can't get enough of *you*. And tonight, when the party's over and everyone is gone and it's just the two of you, he'll prove it." Rosie smiled a wicked, teasing little laugh. "Multiple times, I'll bet."

"Rosemary Bell!" Tammy gasped, raising a hand to cover another laugh.

Rosie grinned and shrugged, taking another sip of her own champagne. It was sweet and delicious, just what the doctor ordered. Rosie smacked her lips, just as Tammy leaned towards her and hastily whispered her next question.

"... did it *hurt?*"

Rosie laugh-coughed, holding her glass aloft as she desperately tried not to spill while also just as desperately trying to stem her laughter because she could tell that Tammy was *serious*.

"I mean," Tammy continued, as Rosie got ahold of herself, "after it's been a while?"

"Not at all," Rosie told her, smoothing her amusement into a kinder form of sisterly affection. "In fact, it felt wonderful! Like coming alive," she sighed. "Like that was how it should have been all along, and not the half-assed effort Randy had used to make."

"Really?" Tammy asked dubiously.

"Really," Rosie promised with a wink.

"Thanks, Rosie," Tammy said warmly, as the two stylists began to drift back towards their posts. "For everything you've done for us since you arrived in town. You're my best friend, and I'm so honored that you're with me today."

"You're *my* best friend," Rosie replied, her eyes starting to feel a little misty. "and I wouldn't dream of being anywhere else...ordinarily. But right now I'm dreaming of a hot shower and a toothbrush."

"Then you'd better scoot," Tammy laughed, dabbing at the corner of her own eyes with the hem of her robe, "while Jennifer and Ellen finish making me fabulous."

"Done and done," Rosie grinned, slipping off her chair with fresh anticipation of using Tammy's fancy bathroom without the risk of the pipes groaning or the water suddenly turning cold the way it sometimes did at Fox Cottage.

CHAPTER TWELVE

Rosie was primped and made up to within an inch of her life, and she couldn't even begin to imagine how Tammy must feel. The dresses, while gorgeous, weren't exactly made from forgiving material and the pair of them climbed stiffly into Tammy's neat little sedan with slow and deliberate movements. The last thing anyone needed was a split seam when they were T-minus fifteen minutes from Tammy walking down the aisle.

All of the preparations for the wedding had been made the night before. Offers of help had dwindled closer to the wedding, especially the more Matthew Bishop became a topic of controversy. Tammy may have been stressed about the implications, but Rosie thought she was glad to be more involved herself. Rosie drove the car carefully down the bend of The Crescent, past Myles' house—which Tammy glanced at and then gave a happy little smile.

It was a strangely misty morning, for a day in mid-summer. They continued along The Promenade, descending the gently sloping hill that would carry them almost right up to the steps of the Hand of God Southern Baptist Church. A crowd was still gathered outside, spilling onto the sidewalk. Rosie pursed her lips with annoyance, thinking about how rude it was of all of them to not already be seated inside the Church itself. How was she going to keep Tammy in the car and hidden from view while she herded everyone?

Her phone went off in the console of Tammy's car, as though it had suddenly received signal and delivered several messages. Because the car wasn't going anywhere anytime soon, she lifted the phone to lazily see what had been delivered.

Rosie. Pick up.
Have you left yet?
Call me before you get to the church.

Rosie knitted her brows. Shouts distracted her from her phone, and the crowd finally broke up enough for her to pull forward around the curve to the church.

"Oh my God," Tammy blasphemed in a horrified breath.

Flames rose high into the air, engulfing the small steeple and sending up thick clouds of smoke that Rosie had mistaken for mist. She wrenched on the handbrake, cut the engine, and got out of the car as quickly as her dress would allow. The smell of the wooden Church burning was clear as day now—some people were covering their mouths and noses with their hands and a few other people were on their cell phones. A siren could be heard in the distance.

Rosie rushed around to the passenger side of the car, helping Tammy get out. He friend seemed as though she were in a trance; her bright BLUE eyes were locked on the fierce inferno that seemed settled on destroying the Church good and proper. Tears bloomed in the corners of Tammy's eyes, and Rosie wrapped an arm around her shoulders as they both realized that the wedding absolutely wouldn't be going ahead as planned.

Any thought of the blaze being an accident was wiped clean off the slate by the huge black pentagram that had been sprayed across the Church's quaint double doors. There was more graffiti sprayed across the front and sides of the building—words, though Rosie couldn't make them out. And to add insult to injury, the area around the front steps was littered with empty and smashed up beer bottles.

"Tammy!" someone shouted.

Rosie looked in the direction of the voice and saw Myles, dressed to perfection in his light grey wedding suit, rushing towards them through the crowd. His hair, which was normally tamed into a pompadour, was bristling up in the wind as though possessed and he had a dark smudge of soot across one cheek.

"Heavens above," he gasped as he reached them, out of breath. He reached for Tammy, bending to look into her tear-streaked face. "Honey, I'm so sorry," he told her, before folding her into a hug.

Rosie stepped away from them, leaving them to commiserate with each other. All around her, the towns-folk of Mosswood who had turned out for the wedding were now instead turned out to witness the destruction of their beloved Church. Her own feelings were a mixed bag, ranging from devastated for Tammy and Myles to sad that the town was losing an icon even if it wasn't a particularly important one to her personally.

And that's when the double doors of the Church burst open to reveal Declan. He had lost his suit jacket and the white button-down shirt he wore had been torn open, buttons missing. The neck of the white t-shirt beneath it had been pulled up to cover his nose and mouth in the best makeshift mask he could produce at a moment's notice. He held a fire extinguisher in one hand, and he barreled out of the burning building with a determination that made Rosie's heart leap into her throat. She rushed over to him.

"Rosie," he said, as though he had forgotten he was less than six feet away from a potentially life-or-death situation. "You look *beautiful*!"

"What the *hell* are you doing in there?!" she shouted, ignoring his compliment and the gasps and glares her blasphemy earned her from the gathered parishioners. "Where are the *kids?!*"

He dropped the fire extinguisher with a dull thunk onto the ash-covered grass by their feet, placing his hands on her upper arms.

"They're fine, darlin'," he promised, his face serious. "Just fine—they're over there—look."

She followed his gazed to where a wide-eyed Maggie stood close to Gabriel on the sidewalk away from the carnage, his arm around her. He was staring at the fire intently, almost as though he looked like he was wishing it would burn hotter. And the good people of Mosswood, it seemed, were torn between staring in disbelief at the blaze and glaring at Gabriel.

"Okay," Rosie conceded, her guts starting to churn with anxiety when she noticed that people were starting to stare at her and Declan, too. "But that doesn't explain why *you* were inside a *burning Church!*"

Declan took a half-step towards her, looking pointedly at the building.

"I was tryin' to see if I could do *somethin'* to put it out," he told her, his words mundane but the slight emphasis he put on the word 'somethin'' telling her he had been trying to use magic. "But it was too far gone. Everythin' inside's already been gutted..."

The gravity of the situation pecked at Rosie's resolve once again. She found that tears were beginning to sting her eyes, and she knew they weren't the result of the smoke swirling around them and engulfing Mosswood.

"It's awful," she whispered, grateful for Declan's strong presence in such a moment.

"I know," he murmured, drawing her close. "It is."

He bent to place a small, reassuring kiss on the crown of her head before guiding them over to where Ben and the kids were standing. Maggie immediately went to her mother, and Rosie folded her into a protective hug.

"Poor Tammy and Myles," Ben said hoarsely a way down the sidewalk. "And poor Mosswood. This is the original Church, built by the town founders. It's a huge loss."

"Yes, it is," growled Earl from the Post Office. He leaned forward so that he was a little apart from the crowd, and glared in the direction of Rosie, Declan, Gabe, and Maggie. "Seems *some* folks around here ain't got no respect for nothin'!"

"Some folks might want to think about goin' to make trouble someplace else," agreed Beverly with a haughty sniff that was hiding her tears.

Gabe looked at Beverly, his eyes narrowed and his jaw set. And then he looked at the other people around her. Some of them had stolen glances at him, but one or two were outright staring. They couldn't have made Beverly's point clearer.

"This is bollocks," he declared. He started for the

truck, kicking up ash with his scuffed Doc Martens as he went.

The sirens got louder until a huge red fire engine slowed down at the curb, waiting for people to move out of the way so that they could pull right up to the building itself. The firefighters didn't waste any time. They had their hose rolled out to start dousing the flames in record time, large clouds of steam rising into the air as well as the smoke. As though to signal that the Church had given up the ghost, the whole left wall of the building collapsed outwards into the small church-yard filled with ancient headstones. The crowd gasped and made loud exclamations.

"Get back! All of y'all!" one of the firefighters yelled at the top of his lungs. The crowd immediately obliged.

"They'll save what they can," Declan said, trying to share his confidence with the rest of them, but it wasn't catching.

Rosie felt any shred of hope she'd been holding onto bottom out. They were the folks these people were referring to. They were no longer welcome in Moss-wood, and the sting of that realization pained Rosie more than she would care to admit. She bit the inside of her bottom lip, deciding that there wasn't much else they could do for the Church.

"Why don't you get Maggie in the truck," she suggested to Declan. "I'm just going to see if I can do anything to help Tammy or Myles, but then we should probably get out of here. All this smoke isn't good."

"Alright love," he replied. "C'mon, Mags." The two of them began to walk to where Declan's truck was parked a little way down the street.

Interest in the event wasn't waning—if anything, the crowd was growing by the minute as word of the fire spread through town. There already wasn't any parking available on the street, but now kids on bicycles and people who had been walking dogs nearby had turned up to rubberneck at the most exciting (and tragic) thing to happen in Mosswood since 'the troubles' had begun.

Myles and Tammy had moved as close to the burning Church as they dared and seemed to be in a prayer circle with a few other members of the congregation, heads bowed and hands joined as they pleaded with God under their breaths. When they broke their circle and the others noticed Rosie, they scattered to the four winds. Rosie approached her friends cautiously, not wanting to intrude.

Tammy's makeup and hair was absolutely ruined, rivers of mascara running rampant down her plump, previously rosy cheeks. Her dress—her perfect wedding gown—was no longer glistening white. Now it was grey with soot and ash, the pearls looking grubby and the fabric ruined, probably forever. Rosie hated the thought of how Tammy would feel when she got home to find that it wasn't just her wedding day that had been ruined, but everything associated with it. Her own heart felt like lead. And that was nothing compared to what her poor, wonderful, darling friend was going to go through.

"I'm so very sorry you guys," she said, pouring out her sympathy as she approached. "Is there anything I can do? Anything at all?"

"Thank you for askin'," Myles replied, his usual friendly politeness replaced with a clipped tone that instantly set Rosie on edge. "But I think I'm just gonna take Tammy on home."

Rosie's gaze slipped to Tammy, who was silently staring at the destruction of her dream wedding. She stepped forward and folded Tammy into a one-sided hug, trying desperately not to be cut to the core by Tammy not hugging her back for the first time ever.

"I'll call later to check in," she murmured to her friend, knowing that Tammy could hear her even if she wasn't ready to deal with the situation unfolding around them. She pulled away without another word, walking in the direction of the truck.

Ben seemed to have taken charge of the situation, and after a curt nod in Myles' direction, he cupped his hands around his mouth to call out across the crowd.

"Okay folks—unfortunately, the wedding's cancelled until further notice. Let's all get on back to our homes now so that these men can do their jobs."

The sun was trying desperately to break through the bank of smoke that was rising into the air, and the day was starting to heat up on its own independently of the fire. A glint of something barely visible in the weak sunshine caught Rosie's eye, and she bent to stare at the ash-clogged grass at her feet. It took her a moment to make sense of what she was seeing, but once she did she felt a wave of nausea crash over her as she bent to pluck the item up out of the grass at her feet.

It was Gabriel's lighter.

THE LIGHTER FELT LIKE IT WAS BURNING A HOLE IN HER dress pocket all the way back to Fox Cottage. Rosie had fallen into a silence just as deep as Tammy's, feeling sick to her stomach and hot all over in a way that had nothing to do with the fire or the weather and everything to do with the culmination of all the events that had happened since Gabe had come smashing into their lives like a wrecking ball.

Rosie slid down from the truck's leather bench seat grabbing Maggie's hand as she followed her mother.

"Family meeting," she declared over her shoulder, her tone allowing for no refusal. "Under the oak tree. *Now*." She marched over to the tree, which stood tall in the middle of the lawn at Fox Cottage. Its huge branches were thick with glossy green leaves that provided welcome relief from the rising sun. Rosie was too worked up to sit down.

She could feel her arcane power almost crackling with electricity—charged with fury. Hovering behind her, she met Declan's confused and hurt expression with one of stony resignation when she turned on the gathered few.

"What's goin' on?" he asked Rosie, but she simply shifted her gaze to Gabriel. He hesitated, as though he didn't wish to get too close to the tree that provided their shelter and shade.

Rosie glared at him for a few seconds, before deciding she was sick of beating around the bush around.

"What did you do, Gabriel?" she asked, quietly. Her tone was the undercurrent of her aura, which she knew full and well every single person around her could feel. When Gabe didn't answer her immediately, Rosie slipped her hand into the pocket of her gown and retrieved the lighter. She tossed it to him, where the sooty grime from the fire that covered it then coated Gabriel's hands, staining them black.

Declan breathed, holding out one hand to stop the conversational horse from bolting. "Rosie? Where'd you get that?"

"At the church," Rosie quirked a brow in Gabe's direction, begging him to contradict her. "Where your son must have dropped it."

Gabe curled his lip up at Rosie in disgust "That's rich, coming from you."

Rosie dipped her chin. "Excuse me?"

"You want to talk about *finding* things?"

Shaking his head with disbelief, Gabe moved over to the trunk of the oak tree. He held out a hand to the bark, and for a second Rosie thought he meant to stroke it. But his hand—and then his arm, and then his whole *body*—disappeared inside of the fairy tree, the magical treaty Rosie had made with the tree shimmering like liquid silver as he vanished.

"What the—?" Rosie gaped at Declan and Maggie.

She barely had time to contemplate how Gabe had even found or entered the tree in the first place when he reemerged from its wizened, gnarled trunk clutching something heavy to his chest. He took two steps away from the tree before flinging it into the dirt of the garden bed, right at Maggie and Rosie's feet.

Rosie felt the blood drain from her face as she recognized the centuries-old leather-bound book that she had told Maggie she could keep as her very own grimoire.

"You said the new rules included no secrets," Gabe growled, his eyes glistening with unshed tears. He turned his head to blink them away, before focusing back on the three people standing on the other side of the grimoire. "But I guess that doesn't apply to you guys, huh?"

Her throat was so dry that she couldn't swallow, so Rosie let her gaze fall to her daughter instead.

Maggie chewed the inside of her cheek, her eyes trained on the grimoire. "I wrote in there about Gemma," she confessed in a small voice.

Regret, pain, and sadness rose up inside of Rosie like a rip tide in a storm. She looked to Gabe, who was staring them all down with a tear he hadn't managed to catch rolling down his cheek until he angrily swiped it away.

Declan stepped towards Gabe, hand outstretched in sympathy. "We were going to tell you," he said gently. "When the time was right."

Gabe stumbled back, out of Declan's reach. "Well maybe I'll tell you about what happened at the Church *when the time is right,"* he snarled.

"We're sorry about what happened with your mom." Rosie looked from Gabe, to Maggie, and then to Declan. When she met locked eyes with Gabe again, his gaze was white hot. "It was wrong of us to keep it from you," she admitted, "and we obviously need to talk about it all. But none of that makes your actions okay. We didn't bail you out so you could add arson to the list."

"You didn't bail me out of anything," Gabe shot back, "my dad did."

It was an insult that would have hit its mark once upon a time, but now it rolled off Rosie the way water rolled downhill.

"Well I can guarantee you that he doesn't have the money to do it a second time," she pointed out.

Gabe's sandy blonde brows arched and he reached into his back pocket, pulling out the crumpled, soot-stained emancipation papers that Declan had thrown into the fireplace in their bedroom.

"So sign this," he spat, waving the documents in

Declan's direction, "and then I'm not your problem anymore."

Declan sighed and pinched the bridge of his nose. "I'm not signing anythin'."

"Then I'm not staying here another second." Gabe set his jaw, ramming the papers back into his pocket as he stormed off towards the house. Silence descended on the trio still standing beneath the oak tree, until Declan broke it.

"I don't think this is working either," he conceded helplessly, his eyes skipping frantically between Rosie's. "I need t'take care of this. I need to take care of *him*."

Rosie felt like a lightning bolt had just struck her heart. She locked eyes with Declan, her thoughts a panicked maelstrom in her head. *Holy shit, what was happening?*

"What exactly are you saying?" she asked breathlessly, already dreading the answer.

Declan's face hardened. "Look, it's like you said. Maybe he needs to be in a more familiar place for a while." He shrugged, glancing at Maggie and then in the direction of Fox Cottage before he forced himself to look back at Rosie. "Maybe when everythin's more settled, we can try all this again."

He stepped forward, enveloping Rosie in a brief hug. His arcane energy mingled with hers for a moment, and then he retreated to give Maggie a hug too. And then his long legs were carrying him across the lawn, away from the both of them.

Rosie was frozen to the spot, staring blankly at the space that both Forrest men had just passed through on their way out of hers and Maggie's lives. And then, after another heartbeat, she felt Maggie's small hand slip into hers.

ROSIE HADN'T REALIZED HOW MUCH SHE HAD BECOME used to the organized chaos of having too many people stuffed into too small of a home until they were all gone. Fox Cottage had played host to Declan, and then Tammy, and then Gabe, and Rosie had almost forgotten how quiet the place was when Maggie was reading in her room and all the household chores were done. Ordinarily she would have been longing for some alone time. But time alone meant time with her thoughts, and they were all snarled up like hurricane grass in a chain link fence.

She padded outside on bare feet, only just able to stand the sun-heated porch steps until she reached the warm but welcoming lawn. Rosie flopped onto the porch swing inelegantly, letting it take her weight and then rock backwards with a creak that sounded something like a sigh. When she felt her thoughts threatening to turn to pondering Declan and Gabe, she dug her cell phone out of the back pocket of her denim cut-off shorts.

Chatting to Tammy always managed to make her feel like everything was less of a shitstorm than she'd imagined, and she really wanted to make sure that she was okay after the disaster the day before. But when Tammy didn't pick up the way she usually did after the third ring, Rosie frowned a little. The expression deepened when Tammy didn't pick up at all. She stared at the screen of her phone, sadness seeping through the handset and up her arm until it reached her heart. Tammy had *never* skipped a call from her before.

Rosie had walked the path to the clearing so many times that she knew it like the back of her hand—or she thought she did. Today things felt a little different. There were none of the small yellow-winged butterflies that usually skipped through the fringes of the long summer grass, and the breeze that always kissed the trees in Needlepoint Woods was woefully absent. The result was hot, heavy air that was full of moisture, sticking to her like glue as she made her way through the trees.

She was only halfway to the clearing when she realized why she was headed there. Aside from being her destination of choice for her monthly moon ritual, the place was sacred to her family. Declan's trailer had been burned by Randy there, and they had defeated Gemma there when she'd tried to hurt Maggie. Rosie had run through there with Declan in hot pursuit, and its where they had gone to give Maggie her first real magic lesson.

And then she remembered the night of Gabriel's teen thrasher—the music, the drinking, and the bonfire. The earth would be scarred once again, charred and dead in the place where he and his friends had shown so much disrespect for pretty much everything. With a sharp inhalation of breath Rosie's steps grew quicker. At least healing the clearing would give her something to do, especially when she couldn't heal so many other things that needed fixing.

She pushed through the last of the trees and out into the long grass of the clearing, her eyes searching for the huge black patch of ashes. But she couldn't see it. Frowning, Rosie padded across the grass in search of the bonfire scar. The linkage of this fire and the one at the Church wasn't lost on her and Rosie was frowning when she reached the spot, only to find that there was no wind for her sails when she got there.

A bright green circle of fresh new shoots of grass reached skyward from the ashen soil, almost completely obscuring any trace of the fire. Surprised, Rosie reached out with her magical aura. She didn't know at first exactly what she was hoping to feel, but when she felt the magic that still lingered around the new grass she pulled her hand back with a gasp.

The magic had been hot, just like the fire that had burned there before it had been conjured. It was chaotic, and unruly, and angry... but there had been more to it there beneath the surface of the spell. Rosie let herself fall gently forward onto her knees, embracing the earth as it surrounded her. She delved deeper with her own magic, uncovering the ripples of hurt and sadness of the magic Gabriel had left behind. But there, like a river beneath all of that, was a long-flowing current of loneliness. And then, with a very thin veneer, she felt the very moment she had taught him this spell, that night after they drenched the yard cleaning up the poop prank.

Rosie leaned forward so that the heels of her palms were resting on his beautiful new grass, and she remembered what it had been like growing up without knowing who her parents were or why they hadn't wanted her. She remembered how it had felt when Declan had told her about her magic, and how hopeless she had felt trying to learn how to control it when there was always another crisis looming around the corner. And it was easy to remember all those feelings, because she could feel them right there in Gabriel's magic, too.

She didn't know how long she sat there, just absorbing Gabriel's magic while it spoke to her own. But, at length, she stood up and dusted the dirt and ashes from her knees. Gabriel was messed up. He was angry, and did stupid things, and hurt the people around him. But he was family. She could feel it in her magic, and now Rosie could feel it in her heart, too. Her Mosswood family would have to make their own choice, but for her part, she chose Gabe and forgiveness. And if she had to choose sides, then she chose Maggie, Declan, Gabriel and herself, even against the world.

Rosie started back for Fox Cottage, her old fire and determination flowing through her veins. She only hoped that she wasn't too late to make things right.

CHAPTER THIRTEEN

"C'mon mom!" Maggie called, cantering down The Ridge towards the highway like a thoroughbred hopped up on oats. She kicked up her heels, unphased by the sweltering heat of the middle of summer's day by a hot asphalt road.

"I'm—going—" Rosie huffed, limping along at a fast walk, behind her, "—as—fast—as—" she gasped, "—I—can."

Maggie doubled back, scurrying up the slope to Rosie with energy that briefly made Rosie think that youth was wasted on the young. "We have to hurry!"

"I know," Rosie puffed, "but it's been—a while—since I did—track." She stopped for a short break, pressing her fingertips gingerly into her side where a stitch had started to develop during the couple minutes she had dared to jog.

"Just breathe in through your nose, and out through your mouth," Maggie instructed. "Like this!"

Maggie flared her nostrils for maximum air intake, tilting her head back and widening her eyes in an expression that was eerily reminiscent of The Rock's signature catch-phrase bit. And then she huffed all the air out of her mouth in one big explosion, making Rosie blink and wonder when Maggie had last brushed her teeth.

"I'll keep that—in mind," Rosie said, raising a brow and thinking that just getting her breath *back* would be a good place to start. After a couple more seconds, she gave in to the urgency of the situation. "Okay," she grimaced, straightening. "Let's go."

Rosie doubled her efforts, letting gravity help her down the slight incline towards the highway while simultaneously praying that she wouldn't slip on the loose gravel by the side of the road and wind up with gravel rash all along her backside. By the time they reached the sugar mill, they had a clear view of the Beep'n'Sleep across the road. A battered-looking yellow cab was parked out front of Maude's office, and Rosie and Maggie watched as Declan put a suitcase in the trunk, closed it, and then disappeared into the back of the car.

"It's them!" Maggie wailed. "We're gonna miss them!"

She moved to dash across the highway, and Rosie's arm shot out to grab her daughter and hold her back.

"Wait!" she said sharply to Maggie, before grabbing her hand and checking both ways for traffic. Seeing none, the pair of them dashed across the road together.

"Stop!" Rosie yelled as loudly as she could, watching Declan and the driver buckling up their seatbelts. The car gave a tiny jolt forward as the drive removed the parking brake and put the car into gear. As soon as Rosie and Maggie reached the other side of the highway safely, Rosie dropped Maggie's hand and made the sprint of her life. She hit the hood of the car with her hands just before the driver stepped on the gas, shocking him into stepping on the brake.

"Rosie?!" Declan exclaimed. He stepped out of the taxi, staring at her incredulously. "What on earth—"

She continued gasping, her shoulders sagging with relief when she saw Gabriel stand up behind the other taxi door, watching her curiously.

Maggie trotted up next to her. "Just give her a moment," she said, placing a hand on her mother's back. "Mom's a bit out of shape."

Rosie glared at her daughter for a brief moment, albeit one in which she was still very much gasping. Then, she moved around to the side of the car.

"You guys," she breathed, still trying to catch up after her last-ditch effort to reach them in time. "Don't go. I'm *so* sorry. For everything!"

Declan and Gabe turned to look at each other. Declan stepped out from behind his door and shut it behind him. Gabe folded his arms on top of the car roof as he looked across at Rosie.

"Just please hear me out," she said, lifting a hand. "I was wrong. When I tried to teach Maggie what to do when she disagreed with someone she loved, I taught her to act with love instead of anger and lies. But when I had the chance to do that for you, I didn't do those things." She looked at Declan, emotion welling behind her eyes. "And I didn't tell you to approach the situation that way, either." Declan clenched his jaw and released it, holding his emotions back, too.

Rosie turned back to Gabriel. "When I had a problem with how my family was changing, I treated you like *you* were the problem, instead of acting like there was a problem and we could all solve it together," she said. She shrugged her shoulders weakly. "It was wrong, and I'm sorry. I'm not perfect, either."

Gabe nodded shortly, accepting her apology. "Okay," he said. His head fell back and he looked at Rosie speculatively down the bridge of his nose—decidedly smaller and pointier than his father's. *Something he inherited from his mother,* Rosie thought guiltily.

"But there has to be no more lying about stuff," he stipulated, "and from now on if you have something you needs to say then you say it, instead of pretending it's not happening."

"Deal." Rosie glanced from him to Declan. "I wanna try and solve this *together*, if y'all are willing to try. Because that's what families do, right? And if you'll still have me, then I want Maggie and I to be your family."

Declan smiled at her, his eyes softening and going a little misty as well. Rosie felt her heart warm up, but she stopped the moment from progressing too much.

"But you will both have to start acting like a family, too. And that means telling the truth," she added, "and pulling each other up when someone goes too far." She looked between Declan and Gabe hopefully, and added sheepishly, "Even if it's me."

Declan looked at Gabe, who took a deep breath and then released it.

"Well, I like the last bit," he admitted, the beginnings of a shy smile catching hold of his face. For the first time Rosie could appreciate the cute way his nose turned up at the end, and the dimple he had in his cheek —the same as his dad.

"Aye," Declan agreed, his easy-going smile making a come-back. "Reckon that sounds like a good way forward."

"Yay!" Maggie squealed, dashing forward and launching herself at Gabe. "Group hug!"

Rosie and Declan rounded the back of the car to join in, wrapping their arms around their kids and leaning over the tops of Maggie and Gabe's heads to share a grateful kiss.

"Are y'all still goin' to Atlanta, or not?" the cabbie called, clearly worried about his fare.

"Not," Declan called back before showing Rosie and the kids a comedic faux-grimace. "Sorry!"

"Damned Mosswood," the cabbie murmured, cutting the engine to wait for the luggage to be unloaded.

"IT WAS JUST ME AND MATTHEW," GABE CONFESSED, later that night when they were all sitting around the kitchen table at Fox Cottage like they had never left it. Rosie, Maggie, and Declan were all listening to Gabe's story unfold with bated breath, only interrupted by the crunch of Maggie every so often stuffing a handful of popcorn into her face.

"We'd been racking our brains for something to do to stop the wedding," he continued, meeting their gazes. "I wanted it to be sneaky, but Matthew wanted to make a big scene. We got to the Church and decided to vandalize it—just a little," he added hastily, as Rosie frowned.

"Ya can't just vandalize something a *little*," Declan admonished, his expression disappointed.

"I guess," said Gabe, looking down at his hands. He flexed and then unflexed them, as though wondering how he had managed to let them cause so much trouble. "I spray-painted the doors and the other stuff on the sides, while Matthew threw our empty beer bottles at the Church building. That's all we were going to do at first, I swear."

Declan lifted his chin at Gabe. "Then what happened?"

Gabe's expression turned bleak. "Matt started throwing the full beer bottles, too. He started yelling at the church and saying how much he hated it. I didn't know what to do about it."

He glanced between Rosie and Declan's riveted stares, and then took a steadying breath. "Then, Matthew asked to borrow my lighter to light his smoke. But when I asked for it back he just kinda laughed. And then he threw it at the church."

"That's how the fire started," Rosie said gently.

Gabe nodded sadly. "It got really big *really* fast. I tried to kick sand at it, but there's not much sand there and we didn't know where we could get any water. And then the fire kind've just... took over." He hung his head, genuinely ashamed of himself. "We got scared. So we ran."

The room was silent after the story was finished. Eventually, Rosie was the first to speak.

"Thank you for being honest," she said, reaching out across the table to take Gabriel's hand. "I know it's not easy, but now that we know what happened we can start to set this right."

"I should have come and told you guys," Gabe admitted, "or called the cops. Or *something*." His voice sounded hollow. "I'm sorry."

Declan reached out to clap a hand onto his son's

shoulder. "Well, we can't change that now," he said, "but we do need a plan goin' forward."

Maggie looked from Gabe, to Declan, and finally to her mom. "When you do something wrong, you have to make it right," she parroted her mother's lesson from a few weeks before. She glanced between them all again.

"Any ideas?" she asked no one in particular.

"WHAT ARE WE GONNA DO IF THEY SLAM THE DOOR IN our faces?" Maggie asked in a small voice. Declan glanced across at Rosie, his usually cheerful face creased with concern as they waited for the door to be answered. He was obviously in the 'door slammed in our faces' camp. Rosie looked at Gabe, whose face was unreadable.

"I'm more worried that they won't open the door at *all*," she admitted quietly, her fingers curled into tense fists inside of her jeans pockets where nobody could see them.

"We'll cross that bridge if we get to it," Declan said tersely, reaching to grab Maggie's hand protectively.

They were rewarded with the sound of footsteps approaching the door. Several locks turned, and then the door itself was pulled gently open to reveal Myles standing there wearing chinos and a pale grey button-down shirt beneath a plastic-coated apron that bore the words 'Kiss the cook if you love Jesus!' complete with a

SON OF A WITCH

huge print of bright red lips on the left breast. He flushed when he noticed just who was standing on his stoop.

"Oh," he said awkwardly, eyes travelling slowly over the assembled group. "Hi, everyone."

Tammy came bustling into the foyer from the direction of the kitchen.

"Who is it Myl—" she began, and then skidded to a halt on the hall rug when she saw the whole gang assembled in the doorway.

Both of them were so pale that Rosie thought for a second that maybe Maggie was right about the door.

"Hi," she began in a rush, wanting to at least get a few words in before they were all left eating Tammy's exquisite summer door wreath. "Look. We're here to apologize and explain, if you've got a minute."

"Please don't slam the door in our faces, Aunt Tammy," Maggie pleaded. She turned hopeful eyes on Tammy, who took a second to process everything and then softened like butter at a picnic on a warm day.

"Of course, I won't slam the door in your faces," she sighed emphatically, bending down and opening her arms. Maggie dropped Declan's hand and rushed to her, scooting past Myles across the invisible line in the sand that had been drawn between the two families. Tammy folded Maggie into a tight hug, bending to kiss the top of Maggie's head. When she straightened to look at Rosie, there were tears glistening in her eyes.

Myles glanced at Tammy, and then stepped out of

203

the doorway to let Rosie, Declan, and Gabe pass. "Y'all had better come in," he said, a hint of kindness returning to his tone.

"Thank you," Rosie sighed gratefully, moving inside before either Myles or Tammy could change their minds. "But there's a few people missing who ought to be here."

Myles looked up, meeting her gaze. After a moment, he nodded. "I'll make some calls."

A little over half an hour and a round of Tammy's famous lemonade later everyone who needed to be present was gathered, except for two people. Rosie, Declan, Maggie and Gabe were seated on the sectional by the large windows that looked out onto Myles' leafy front yard. Tammy was in an armchair by the unused fireplace, Myles perching on the arm of her chair. Ben was in the other armchair, looking distinctly uncomfortable. The doorbell rang, but whoever had pressed it let themselves in instead of waiting for the door to be answered.

"What on earth was so important?" Prissy's voice echoed disdainfully from the foyer. "I was in the middle of my evening prayer routine!" She came around the corner into the living room, freezing when she noticed the crowd assembled before her. A heartbeat later Matthew appeared in the doorway behind her.

"We won't take up any more of your time than we have to," Rosie promised tersely, crossing her legs.

Prissy opened up her mouth to say something, but

then seemed to think better of it. Rosie wondered if there was some kind of cosmic imbalance in the air— Prissy exercising self-restraint wasn't exactly *normal*.

"Gabe," Declan said gently, turning to his son. He nodded encouragingly, and Gabe took a breath before he stood up.

Matthew watched him with wide eyes, going a little pale. "What are you doing?" he asked, panicked.

Gabe set his shoulders. "What we should have done the night of the fire."

He told the whole room what he had already told his dad, Maggie, and Rosie—right up to the part where Matthew had lit the fire with his lighter. Prissy looked scandalized that her son was smoking cigarettes, but Myles was able to look past that and right into the heart of the problem.

"But *why*, son?" he asked, his face sadder than Rosie had ever seen it.

"Yes!" Prissy chimed in. "Why would you embarrass us like this?"

Matthew pulled a face at his mother's word, as though she had hit the nail on the head. "Because you all care more about that stupid Church than you do about *me!*" he declared hotly. "Growin' up all I ever heard about was what needed doin' down there. I knew that building better than I knew my own house!"

Myles got up, crossing the room to where Matthew had perched himself on the piano stool. He placed a hand on his son's shoulder and squeezed.

"*Nothing* means more to us—both of us—than you do, Matthew." Myles looked to his ex-wife for support.

All eyes shifted to Prissy the way people follow the ball at a tennis match. But for once, the woman surprised Rosie.

"Of course," she said, moving to sit next to Matthew on the bench. She took Matthew's hand in her perfectly manicured one. "We *both* love you, so much." And then, after a heartbeat, Rosie heard a word she thought she would never hear fall from the mouth of Priscilla Bishop. "We're sorry if we ever made you doubt that."

"We never should've let our own personal struggles with each other get in the way of our bein' good parents," Myles added. "Maybe it would help if I *did* step down as pastor so that I could spend more time with you."

The tide of Matthew's anger finally seemed to wear itself down to a trickle. He hung his head, nodding a little.

"What would really help," he said, his voice thick, "is if you both stopped tryin' to make me decide who I want to live with," he said, looking up at Myles reproachfully before turning his attention to Prissy, "and which parent I like better. I love both of you."

"Of course you do," Myles sighed, tension visibly leaving his body as he pulled Matthew into a rough hug that included Prissy. Rosie's brows lifted at the sight, until Matthew looked past his folks and saw Tammy in the chair across the room. He disentangled himself and walked over to her.

"I didn't know how to handle it when you came into my life, ready to pick up where Mom left off with dad and the Church," he said. For a minute it sounded like he might be ready to start up again with his temper, but then his expression softened some. "But I can see that it was all your way of makin' an effort to fit in with the family. I'm sorry I didn't give you a chance to do that."

He held a hand out to Tammy to shake in friendship, and she took it.

"Oh hon, it's okay," she said, on the verge of a sob. "But 'round these parts, family don't just shake on it. C'mere." She hopped to her feet and hugged Matthew around the middle. He seemed startled, but after a moment he relaxed into it.

"It's not okay," he insisted, ashamed. "I'm so sorry about the church, and your wedding."

"It takes more than that to tear down a church *or* a marriage," Tammy assured him. Her eyes met Rosie's across the room. "Or a friendship." Rosie's heart sparked with love, and she pressed her lips together in a tight, emotional smile that aimed to stop her waterworks from starting up too.

"True enough," she said kindly, nodding at Tammy.

"And we're sorry about your store," Matthew added then, speaking to Ben who had been silent this whole while. Ben took a breath.

"Yeah," Gabe added genuinely. "We really didn't mean to wreck the car. It just sort of... happened."

The two boys looked at each other and then away, and several pairs of parental eyeballs picked up on it at once.

"*What* happened?" Rosie asked suspiciously.

Matthew looked at Gabriel. Gabriel looked at Matthew. Matt was the first to speak.

"We sort of thought we saw..." Matt glanced at Gabe again, and then came out with it. "A kangaroo."

"In the street," Gabe added helpfully.

"A kangaroo?" Rosie frowned slightly. "In Mosswood?"

"Whatever it was, I tried not to hit it!" Matthew explained. "But then we hit your store instead."

Ben lifted his eyebrows. He stared into the middle distance as though searching for something to say. "Well," he offered at last. "That sounds like an accident to me. And I'm pretty sure my insurance covers accidents."

"Well," Tammy sniffled, pleased. "If this ain't the phoenix risin' up out of the ashes!"

Prissy pulled a face at the optimism. "Well, I had better *rise up* and head home," she snipped primly. "I left all my lights on, rushin' over here. Coming, Matthew?" She glanced at her son, who looked between his parents.

"Stayin' here," he said eventually. "Thanks, Mom."

"Alright," Prissy said, as though trying to come to

terms with everything in the light of the evening's revelations. "Well. Goodnight!" Her voice was still huffy as she said her farewell, but there was something different about the way the woman left that caught Rosie's eye. As though perhaps the chip she usually wore on her shoulder had been replaced with something a little more like a conscience.

Everyone wandered back to their seats, the mood in the room finally feeling as though it had unburdened itself. But there was still a little niggle in Rosie's stomach that wouldn't let up, and she figured that now was as good a time as any to voice it.

"I'm glad we've all come back together," she said hesitantly, "and I don't want to be the one who points out the obvious."

"But?" Declan asked her, suspiciously.

"But," Rosie continued, glancing around the room at her chosen family. "I don't know that the town will be ready to just up and forgive everything that's happened so easily." She thought back to the angry voices of Earl and his crew that day at Nourish, and the glares that had been directed at her, Maggie, Declan and Gabe during the fire at the Church. Everyone fell into a moment of hushed contemplation, but it was Ben who finally broke through it.

"Well," he said slowly, the idea forming in his mind. "Mosswood was founded around that original Church, back in the day." His boyish grin fell into place. "Don't see why we couldn't build it up again the same way."

CHAPTER FOURTEEN

The next morning, the whole group reassembled on the curb outside the charred remains of the Hand of God Southern Baptist Church. The fire had gutted the entire place. All the walls were missing, with huge lumps here and there that had used to be pews or kitchen appliances. By some miracle, the frame of the Church was still standing, but it looked like a charcoaled chicken frame that had been left on the barbecue all summer long. One by one, everyone in the group leaned to peer at Ben who chewed the inside of his cheek thoughtfully.

"Okay, it's worse than I thought," he conceded.

"I'll admit that it doesn't look promisin'," Myles said, his hopeful tone contradicting his words. Matthew snorted, and even as Myles began to speak his next words, his son spoke along with him in mockingly chipper tone, until Myles stopped speaking altogether to let Matthew do his best Pastor Bishop impersonation.

"But nothin' does, until you put a little love into it!" The teen bent his arm in front of himself in a cheesy 'aw shucks' gesture, pulling a snort from Declan.

Myles nodded serenely. "What he said," he agreed.

"Where do we even start?" Rosie asked. It looked like a massive job, and she wasn't even sure that they should be working under a frame that looked as though it could collapse any minute.

"We need to clear up all the ashes and fallen debris first," Myles announced, rolling up his sleeves, ready to take charge, "and then we can check how stable the rest of the structure is."

"Don't worry," Declan murmured in Rosie's ear, as though he could read her thoughts. "I reinforced those beams with magic myself earlier. They're not comin' down anytime soon."

"Okay," Tammy said, glaring at the huge mess as though she was about to finish it like leftover pumpkin pie at Thanksgiving. "Let's get to work."

Matthew and Gabe grabbed shovels that had been brought along for the purpose and began to shovel ashes into wheelbarrows that Myles and Ben had brought with them. Declan and Ben pushed the barrows over to the trailer that Ben had hitched up to the back of Declan's truck. It didn't take long to fill it up, and everyone got back to work scraping up piles of more ashes while

Declan and Gabe drove off to get rid of the first trailer-load.

Tammy, Rosie and Maggie swept in the wake of scraping, but the floors had been burned right down to the cement foundation.

"I don't know if loosing that linoleum is a blessing or a curse," Tammy confessed with a sheepish smile to Rosie as they worked.

"A blessing," Rosie replied with certainty, making Tammy giggle.

Declan and Gabe had just left to go haul another trailer load of ashes when Matthew came over to take up Tammy's broom for a bit to give her a break. Rosie smiled at him encouragingly, and he threw her a sheepish look in return. He turned to say something to Maggie, stopped, and then blinked in the direction of the street.

"Hey," he said quietly. "Check it out."

Rosie, Tammy, and Maggie all looked over to where another truck and trailer combo had parked. Earl from the Post Office climbed out, looking a little worse for wear but his gait was determined as ever. Matthew handed Tammy back her broom and wandered over, and after a short exchange with Earl he began to shovel another pile of ashes into the trailer.

But another surprise was wandering up the lawn towards the women, tray carefully balanced in hand.

"Looks like thirsty work," Beverly Brown said politely. "Would y'all like some lemonade?"

"Yes please," Maggie announced, dropping her broom immediately. Beverly smiled and handed her a cup.

"That's mighty kind of you, Mrs. Brown," Tammy cooed. "It's hotter'n blue blazes out here. Thanks."

"Yes, thanks Mrs. Brown" Rosie chimed in, brushing her sweaty bangs back out of her face and gratefully accepting an ice cold drink. Before long, Matthew and Earl had joined them.

"You know," Beverly said, the wheels in her mind turning as she collected up everyone's cups. "I used to know a thing or two about scrubbing floors. I'm just gonna run on home for my favorite brush. Be right back!"

"Favorite brush?" Rosie asked Tammy from the side of her mouth, as Beverly hurried off home.

"Let's not look gift cleaners in the mouth," Tammy whispered back.

Over the course of the afternoon, the ashes were cleared, the fallen debris was picked up, and everything that could be swept or scrubbed was attended to. One by one the nearby residents of Mosswood joined in the effort; from Carol-Ann and Maude trimming back the burned bushes in the gardens to the Minetti family from the local Italian restaurant showing up with more buckets and scrubbing brushes to clean up the blackened headstones in the cemetery.

By mid-afternoon the whole place really looked much better—more like some kind of strange pergola in the middle of the gorgeous Lee Park than a burned-out building. But prettier than the church was the people surrounding it.

Veronica from the Vet Clinic and her boyfriend Joey were chatting happily with Maude and Earl. Myles looked like he was getting a pep talk from Carol-Ann, and Rosie smiled to see Maggie with Declan and Granny, who had just arrived from the Diner with boxes and boxes of free hotdogs for the troops.

Tammy stood next to Rosie and the pair just watched the scene unfold for a few minutes. And then Tammy linked their arms together.

"This is incredible," Tammy said, turning to Rosie with tears glistening in her eyes. "And it isn't even magic."

Rosie smiled, and bumped Tammy companionably to cheer her up. "Sure it is," she said, smiling at the community spirit that filled the area from top to bottom. "It's just a different *kind* of magic, is all." And then Rosie was struck with an idea.

"In fact," she said slowly, letting inspiration build in her mind as she turned to Tammy excitedly. "There are lots of different kinds of magic!"

"Okay," Tammy said slowly, looking at Rosie suspiciously. "Why're you lookin' at me like the cat that got the cream?"

Rosie leaned into her friend. "Do you still wanna get married?"

"More than anything," Tammy said breathlessly, with a lightning-fast glance at Myles.

"Then we haven't got any time to waste," Rosie declared, leading them forward. "C'mon!"

THE NEXT AFTERNOON TAMMY AND ROSIE WERE situated back at Tammy's impressive dressing table. Secure in the knowledge that all of their other last-minute plans had been or were in the process of being executed, they were attending to the most important aspect of any wedding: hair and make-up.

"Are you sure this is like... *allowed?*" Tammy asked for what must have been the hundredth time, wriggling slightly on the folding chair she had set up. The mirror was outlined with tiny LED bulbs that had adjustable hues for different skin-tones, and there were enough different make-up products on the table itself to make Rosie feel like a panic-attack was only one extra mascara wand away. Having grown up the way she did, she didn't know a whole lot about make-up. But she did have an ace up her sleeve.

"It's magic, not nuclear warfare," she smirked, secretly relieved that she didn't need to try wading through Tammy's beauty supplies. "I don't know about *you*, but I'd much rather be ready in two minutes than two hours. We just don't have that kind of luxury," she added slyly. "Because *someone* is a little impatient."

"Can you blame me?" Tammy asked airily. "Have you *seen* that man?"

Rosie grinned at her friend in the mirror as she began to draw in her arcane energy, letting it slowly build inside of her. It felt like dust motes dancing serenely in a sunbeam, and for a moment she relished the calm complexity of holding the power together with her will.

"Close your eyes," she said gently, and Tammy obliged.

When Rosie was ready she leaned forward, placing her fingertips on Tammy's brow. She combed them backwards as though meaning to run her fingers through Tammy's hair, letting her magic flow through them as she moved.

A wide, intricate braid began to knit itself into a honey-golden pattern. Tiny peach blossoms began to bloom amongst the loops of hair, nestled perfectly into the style. A few wisps of hair tugged themselves free around Tammy's face, framing her round cheeks delicately. The magic tapered off, leaving an expertly loose chignon at the nape of Tammy's neck that would be the perfect place to pin her veil.

Another whispering breath of magic enveloped Tammy, illuminating her skin and giving it that ethereal bridal glow that so many strived for on their special day. Rosie sought to bring out Tammy's natural beauty rather than plaster her with color. Nude, shimmering lids had a little depth closer to the base of Tammy's naturally dark lashes. Her lips were flushed with a peachy color that bordered on nude itself—lipstick that wouldn't fade all day no matter how many glasses of champagne Tammy drank or how often she kissed her new husband.

"There," she said gently, stepping back with her heart full of pride as she looked at her gorgeous friend. "What do you think?"

Tammy's eyes fluttered open hesitantly, and then widened when she saw the pure, natural beauty in the reflection that stared back at her.

"Rosie," Tammy breathed, turning her head this way and that in the mirror to admire the effect. "It's *perfect!*" The blush in the apples of her cheeks was enhanced by Rosie's magical makeup, and she started to get teary.

"Don't you dare," Rosie warned, only half joking. "We don't have time. Now, go put on that stunning dress of yours and then come back here so I can zip you up."

Tammy's face fell. She had clearly been wanting to stay and watch Rosie literally work her magic. "But—"

"You're not the *only* one who needs hair and makeup, Tammy," Rosie replied loftily, winking at Tammy she leaned into the mirror to get herself ready. "Shoo!"

CHAPTER FIFTEEN

The whole town turned out for the wedding-that-almost-wasn't. By the time Rosie made her way to the beautiful lace pattern that Gabe had hastily sprayed onto the concrete foundation to serve as an aisle, she could see all the familiar faces of Mosswood—and then some. Everyone had banded together to bring chairs in for the occasion, resulting in a delightfully shabby-chic mashup of furniture styles topped with sprigs of wildflowers that Maggie and Carol-Ann had collected from the firefly meadow.

In hindsight, Rosie thought as she walked serenely towards the temporary altar, the burning down of the Church could be seen as something of a blessing in disguise. If they had all attempted to crowd into the building as it *had* been, folks would've had to dangle from the rafters for a view of the ceremony.

It couldn't have been a more perfect day. Blessedly mild with a breeze that fluttered all the white tablecloths the town had managed to bring together on short notice to decorate the frame of what was being called the Old Church. The casual vibe made it feel more like a family affair than a town gathering, even more so because every single person that Rosie loved best in the world was right here with her.

Declan, Gabe and Maggie smiled up at her from their seats in the front row, while she took comfort from Ben's steady presence beside them. Matthew stood tall next to his father in his rightful place as Best Man, the pair of them in charcoal slacks with crisp white shirts open at the collars and rolled up at the sleeves. Wildflower buttonhole arrangements complimented their outfits.

Tammy's wedding aisle song began to play—an upbeat song by Sara Bareilles called *I Choose You.* Her gorgeous peach-to-dusky-pink gown flowed beautifully as she walked, matched her wildflower bouquet perfectly.

When Tammy appeared at the end of the aisle and began her slow walk towards her future husband, Rosie took stock of the twin expressions of pride and love on the faces of her two friends. Tammy glanced gratefully at Rosie—to whom she handed her bouquet of wildflowers mixed with peach-colored roses—and then her eyes never strayed far from Myles.

A tall woman dressed to the nines in a muted steel-blue suit with a string of expensive pearls around her neck smiled brightly at the congregation.

"Good afternoon," she began. "I'm Avery Harland, a good friend of Pastor Bishop's from the Servants of Divine Light Seminary, and I'm thankful to be asked to officiate today." She cleared her throat.

"Dearly beloved, we are gathered here on this *blessed* summer's day to celebrate the union of this man and this woman," she gestured to the happy couple, "in holy matrimony—*finally!*"

A gentle ripple of laughter moved through the congregation. Avery shifted her weight sassily, holding up one hand that held a bunch of index cards as a few people clapped and Myles blushed.

"It's hotter'n a goat in a pepper patch out here, so we're gonna get right down to brass tacks," the minister added, turning to Myles.

"Myles. Do you take this woman to be your wife? To love her, to honor her, to comfort her, and to keep her in sickness and in health, forsaking all others, for as long as you both shall live?"

Myles looked from Avery to Tammy, a wide grin on his handsome face. "I do."

Avery nodded with satisfaction. "And Tammy, do you take this man to be your husband? To love him, to honor him, to comfort him, and to keep him in sickness and in health, forsaking all others, for as long as you both shall live?"

Tammy's expression had initially been serious as she

studied Myles' face. When she didn't answer immediately Rosie felt a thrill of panic bubble up inside of her. But just as she thought Tammy might really be preparing to say *no*, a slow and determined smile blossomed on Tammy's beautiful face.

"I do," she said, giving Myles leave to relax visibly.

He wasn't the only relieved person present. Avery slowly let go of the breath she had been holding, turning back to Myles.

"Repeat after me. I, Myles, take you Tammy to be my wife. To have and to hold from this day forward, for better, for worse, for richer, for poorer, in sickness and in health, to love and to cherish, till death do us part."

Myles' bright blue eyes shone with a hint of emotion that threatened to turn into tears as he repeated his vow.

But Tammy was a little too eager. She seemed to forget that Avery hadn't yet asked *her* to repeat the phrase, and instead took over the ceremony without hesitation. "I, Tammy, take you Myles to be my husband. To have and to hold from this day forward, for better, for worse, for richer, for poorer, in sickness and in health, to love and to cherish, till death do us part."

There was a tiny silence as the congregation paused to work out what had just happened, but Avery laughed it off with aplomb. "Well done," she complimented the bride. "Y'all'll be makin' me obsolete before long!" Tammy flushed sheepishly, but the effect overall was quite charming.

The exchanging of the rings went smoothly—two

simple, beautiful platinum rings were placed exactly where they ought to have been—and Avery got to wrapping things up.

"Myles and Tammy have invited us to share in this celebration as they affirm their love before us, pledge their faith to one another and enter into the joys and privileges of marriage," she said, bringing her hands together to clasp in front of her immaculate suit. "If there is anyone present who can show just cause why these two people may not be joined in matrimony, speak now or forever hold your peace."

As though Fate itself had intervened, at that precise moment a shabby-looking Kombi van pulled up to the curb with a loud bang and a puff of smoke as it back-fired and then shuddered to a complete stop. It was painted in uneven rainbow stripes that made Rosie think instantly of a hippie commune, and everyone at the wedding swiveled to stare as a man with shaggy brown hair and a long beard that intermingled with it hopped out of the drivers' side.

He was dressed in ripped jeans and wrecked Birken-stocks, sporting a bright pink and yellow tie-died shirt that had something written on it. The man flung open the sliding back door of the van and children toppled out one after the other, one handing him a bright yellow acoustic guitar which he slung onto his back like a trou-badour. There were five in all, ranging in age from about twelve down to a little boy who looked about six. There was something very familiar about the man that

Rosie couldn't put her finger on, and she blinked with panic as he rushed down the aisle towards Myles and Tammy with his kids in tow.

"Tammy?" he called. "Tammy Holt?"

Rosie flew to Tammy, determined not to let anyone or anything ruin this day for her friend who had waited long enough for her moment already. As she got to her friend's side Rosie could see that Tammy had gone pale, as though she had just seen a ghost. Myles looked like he was about to throw up, which was even worse. And then Rosie herself recognized the man who was standing in front of Tammy and Myles, keeping them from finalizing their marriage vows.

Her eyes skipped from the man's scraggly face, down to the words 'MAKE LOVE NOT WAR' printed on his tie-died shirt.

"Terry?!" Rosie gasped as he approached, trying to keep quiet even though people were already rubbernecking. "What are you doin' here?" She hesitated a split-second. "And why do you look like a Partridge Family reboot?"

"This is my adopted family—and band!" he declared, confirming Rosie's fears that he had press-ganged a group of children into touring and performing bad music with him.

"Terry?!" Prissy exclaimed loudly, from where she had been standing at the back of the crowd. She was wearing a black dress that had been tailored to within an inch of its tolerance, and had spent the entirety of the

short ceremony dabbing at her eyes with a handkerchief beneath the dramatic black pillbox hat and veil combo she had donned for the occasion. She craned her neck to get a good look at him, and then made a face as though she'd just swallowed a bug. "What was I *thinkin'?*" she wondered, and then pressed a black-gloved hand to her mouth as though shocked she had actually said it out loud.

"Some of us *did* wonder," Rosie quipped before she could help it.

Terry held up his hands as though to surrender. "I don't expect you to understand," he said, turning his attention to Tammy. "I don't expect *any* of you to understand. But... well!" He flapped his arms in a kind of shrug that Rosie supposed they were meant to find charming but which fell really short of the mark. "I just wanted to come and give the happy couple my blessin'!" he added, with a grin that made Rosie want to punch him.

She stepped forward, getting ready to *make* him leave if no one else was going to do the honor, but he scurried out of the way before she could reach him, herding his kids in front of him as he went. Rosie went to follow him, but Tammy was determined to salvage the ceremony.

"It's okay," Tammy said to her, grabbing Rosie's arm to de-escalate the situation. She gestured to Avery, who took the hint immediately.

"By virtue of the authority vested in me under the

laws of the State of Georgia, I now pronounce you husband and wife. You may kiss the bride!"

A few happy sighs went up from the crowd as Myles gently lifted Tammy's veil, blinking as he drank in the sight of her beautiful, happy face. And then he leaned down to place a chaste, Church-appropriate kiss on her lips. But it seemed as though Tammy had other ideas.

Her hands swept up into Myles' hair, disturbing his carefully coiffed pompadour as she deepened their kiss into something that was definitely one-hundred-percent not Church-appropriate. Rosie didn't know whether Tammy was intent on testing the magical all-day lipstick theory or what, but she grinned nevertheless. A couple of the most good-natured people in attendance whooped and wolf-whistled, and when Tammy finally pulled away it was with a coy smile. Myles looked decidedly dazed, as though he'd never been kissed with such passion in his life.

The new Mr and Mrs Bishop beamed at each other and then their guests and began to walk back down the aisle where everyone was waiting to congratulate them. Rosie followed along behind with Matthew, still holding Tammy's bouquet, as the rest of the crew joined her.

ROSIE AND DECLAN RELAXED TOGETHER ON A PICNIC rug in the middle of Lee Park, while the wedding reception buzzed around them. Children ran wild, trying to catch the lightning bugs and steal extra pieces of cake in equal measure. Elladine had done a fabulous job of re-using what she could from the original wedding food in the style of picnic-hampers for guests to share amongst themselves, and the lazy evening atmosphere had been just what everyone had needed after the hard work of getting the Church ready for the wedding.

"Y'know," Declan sighed, leaning back on the palms of his hands, "this whole summer's been *totally* crackers."

Rosie smiled and laid down on the rug so that her head was nestled comfortably in his lap. "Just the summer?" she teased.

"You've a fair point," he smirked down at her. She glanced up at him, his head framed by the deepening night sky. Two tiny stars twinkled just behind his left ear, and she gazed at them in wonder.

"I don't think I would ever want life to be slow and simple," she said.

"That's not what you said a year ago," he reminded her, glancing down with a knowing grin. "Remember?"

"Things change," Rosie smiled back, shrugging a shoulder. "People do too, I guess." She thought about just how much things and people changed, sometimes. Often for the better.

Declan studied her face for a moment. "Are you sure ya don't mind the calamity?"

"Even if *every* day was going to be crackers," she

teased, using his word, "I'd still get out of bed just to spend it with you."

Declan's eyes softened, a smile curving his lips.

"I'm thrilled t'hear it," he said, wriggling to scratch his ear. They paused like that for a minute—Rosie looking up into the majesty of the sky, where the stars began to reveal themselves, and Declan watching the wedding reception.

"Rosemary Bell?" he asked her, his tone suddenly serious.

"Yes, Declan Forrest?" she replied airily, mocking the formality his tone had just adopted.

He held something in front of her face, pinched between his thumb and forefinger. It glittered in the twilight, and a lightning bug zoomed past it so that the deep purple hue of the multifaceted stone in the middle of the ring was momentarily lit up.

"Will you marry me?"

Thanks for reading

Thanks so much for reading Son of a Witch. I hope you enjoyed this latest instalment of the Mosswood series.

The more I delve into this world, the more I fall in love with it. It's such a joy to discover new characters, new situations, and new beginnings - no matter the form they might take! Bringing Gabe into the fold is something I have looked forward to doing since book 1, and now that he's here I'm thrilled to have him as part of the Mosswood family.

The next book in the series, *Witch Way to Salem*, takes Rosie on a very unexpected trip that will challenge her to her very core in a race to beat time itself.

I do hope you'll join her.

Louisa xo

Bless your heart

This book wouldn't be what it is without the support of all my nearest and dearest. Much like Rosie has her amazing chosen family, I am also blessed with a gang of incredible people who keep me keepin' on. Thanks, guys.

Thanks also go to the incredible ladies at a certain nursing home, for always being super excited when my paperback copies arrive. Your joy gives me joy!

Thank you to my editor, Kimberly Jaye, for once again helping me produce the best book I could write.

I wouldn't have written a fifth book if not for my amazing partner and business manager, Lindsay. Thanks for keeping me on track, calming me down, and plying me with seaming hot cups of coffee.

I have to thank my mum, for her never-ending enthusiasm for what I'm doing with my life these days. She's inspired me in more ways than one, and I'm proud to have such a strong and incredible woman in my life.

And lastly, thank you to my beautiful daughter - always and forever.

Love it? Review it!

A reader writing a review for a book is such a gift to an author. Not only does it let us know that someone out there actually read the thing, but it's so heart-warming to think that they enjoyed it enough to offer their thoughts on it afterwards.

If you've enjoyed this book, I would be so grateful if you'd consider leaving me a review! You can do this by searching for the book title and my name on Amazon.com or on GoodReads.com and then following the prompts.

If you're a book-blogger, bookstagrammer, or journalist and you would like to interview me, please get in touch with me at www.louisawest.com - I would love to chat with you!

Your next Mosswood adventure awaits!

WITCH
WAY TO SALEM
MIDLIFE IN MOSSWOOD BOOK 6

Available for preorder on Amazon

https://books2read.com/wwts

Witch Way to Salem

Last Halloween she was as busy as a bat out of hell, but this year is about to drain the life out of her... literally.

Rosemary Bell should be on top of the world. Her Mosswood family has expanded by one step-son, her new business venture is up and running, and she's just received a proposal... until the Council of Witches (who she lovingly refers to as the COW) has something to say about it.

Her and Declan head to Salem, the witch capital of the world, to get the COW's blessing for their engagement--but all is not as it seems. When an evil spell transports Rosie's soul back in time, she's confronted by a world that not only hunts witches, but burns them at the stake too.

In a time fraught with danger, Rosie must find a way back to the present--and her vulnerable family. She will need to escape from the dangers of history and make her way back before time runs out--or risk not having a future at all.

***The Crucible* meets *Back To The Future* in this fang-tastic short novel about learning from the past, strengthening blood ties, and making the most of the time you have.**

PREORDER NOW

https://books2read.com/wwts

MIDLIFE IN
MOSSWOOD

PARANORMAL WOMEN'S FICTION SERIES

LOUISA WEST

Join the coven

Get updates direct to your inbox

Subscribe to my newsletter for updates about new releases, freebies, sales, giveaways and more!

Subscribe

Be part of the community

Join my reader group on Facebook for exclusive member content, giveaways, and access to my fabulous online VIP book launch parties.

Join

Let Amazon do the heavy lifting

Follow me on Amazon to get notified about my new preorders and releases so that you don't miss out on your next fresh read.

Follow

Also by Louisa West

THE MIDLIFE IN MOSSWOOD SERIES

New Witch on the Block

Jealousy's A Witch

We Witch You A Merry Christmas

Get Witch Quick

Son of a Witch

Witch Way to Salem

How the Witch Saved Christmas

Nice Day for a Witch Wedding

TIL DEATH SERIES

Kiss of Death

About the author

Louisa likes Pina Coladas and gettin' caught in the rain. Determined to empty her brain of stories, she loves writing Paranormal Women's Fiction and other stories about kick-ass women doing whatever the hell they want to do.

She lives in Mandurah, Western Australia, and drinks more coffee than is good for her. When she's not writing or researching projects, Louisa enjoys spending time with her family, and Harriet The Great (Dane). Hobbies include playing video games, watching copious amounts of tv, and various craft-related initiatives.

She strongly believes that the truth is still out there.

Are you interested in:

- New release information and pre-order links
- Competitions, giveaways, and other freebies
- Sneak peeks at cover reveals and excerpts
- VIP access to online launch parties and
- Exclusive member rewards

Then join Louisa's online reader group at
www.facebook.com/groups/magicalmayhem!

facebook.com/louisawestauthor

instagram.com/louisa_west

amazon.com/author/louisawest

goodreads.com/louisawest

pinterest.com/louisawestauthor

CPSIA information can be obtained
at www.ICGtesting.com
Printed in the USA
LVHW091935050122
707923LV00006B/116